"Are yo____ queries ____ concern. "You're looking a bit pale. I hope nothing you ate at lunch has upset you."

Gina shook her head. "No, I'm fine. It's just…well, I've had two rather upsetting conversations this afternoon. And to tell you the truth, I don't quite understand what's going on."

"Which is—what?" he asked. But when she didn't immediately reply, he added, "If you have a problem, Gina, then I think you'd better tell me about it."

"It seems our marriage is the problem," she declared, looking him straight in the eye.

MARY LYONS was born in Toronto, Canada, moving to live permanently in England when she was six, although she still proudly maintains her Canadian citizenship. Having married and raised four children, her life nowadays is relatively peaceful—unlike her earlier years when she worked as a radio announcer, reviewed books and, for a time, lived in a turbulent area of the Middle East. She still enjoys a bit of excitement, combining romance with action, humor and suspense in her books whenever possible.

Books by Mary Lyons

Mary Lyons

THEIR CONVENIENT MARRIAGE

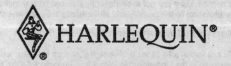

TORONTO • NEW YORK • LONDON
AMSTERDAM • PARIS • SYDNEY • HAMBURG
STOCKHOLM • ATHENS • TOKYO • MILAN • MADRID
PRAGUE • WARSAW • BUDAPEST • AUCKLAND

ISBN 0-373-12167-9

THEIR CONVENIENT MARRIAGE

First North American Publication 2001.

Copyright © 2000 by Mary Lyons.

PROLOGUE

IT WAS always the same dream...

The plaza in Seville is ringing with the loud shouts and whistles of the bystanders. She is almost deafened by the noisy, blaring trumpets and drums of the brass bands as the cavalcade of many horses and their riders, all in traditional Spanish costume, make their way slowly through the crowded throng of spectators.

She is struggling to control a high-spirited, nervous horse, perspiration running down her frightened cheeks as she clings tightly to the thin leather reins, helplessly unable to prevent her mount from either rearing up or lashing out with its hind hooves. The scowling faces and muttered oaths of the other riders are causing her face to burn with shame and humiliation. She knows it will only be minutes...seconds...before disaster strikes.

And then...he is there! His tall and handsome figure, clothed in a black matador's costume, is racing through the milling crowd towards her. Firmly grasping hold of her horse's reins, he turns to smile up at her as she slips out of the saddle and down into his arms, weeping with relief while clinging tightly to the strength of his hard, firm body.

Suddenly, the scene changes and they are dancing...spinning...whirling to the throbbing music of guitars. She is aware of nothing but the hypnotic beat of clapping hands and the rapid 'click-clack' of their

5

heels on the floor as he swirls her about his tall, dominant figure.

Totally mesmerised by the glinting warmth in his eyes, she finds herself being dragged from the dance floor, her hand firmly clasped in his as they run laughing through the empty, deserted streets, before he hails a horse-drawn carriage. And then, within the confined darkness of the vehicle, with shafts of moonlight illuminating his high cheekbones and dark gleaming eyes, he slowly takes her into his arms and she ardently raises her lips to meet his.

She is shivering and trembling with delight at his deepening kiss, quivering at the sensual touch of his hands sweeping over the soft curves of her body. Her emotions are spiralling completely out of control as she whispers, 'I love you, Antonio. I love you with all my heart!'

But then…with shocking suddenness…she finds herself on the other side of the carriage.

'At your age? What can you know of love?' he grinds out savagely, his voice sounding harsh and strained as the vehicle comes to a halt. Swearing under his breath, he pushes her out of the carriage in front of him.

'Go home to England! Go home. Grow up. And let us both forget that this incident ever happened!' he adds grimly, before stalking ahead of her into the house and quickly disappearing from sight.

Totally shattered, and weeping as if her heart will break in two, she stands gazing after him, her eyes blind with tears as she realises that she will never, ever see him again.

It was always the same dream…the same nightmare…

CHAPTER ONE

'I REALLY can't understand why you are being so stubborn, Antonio. Surely you can see that it's the perfect solution to all your problems?'

'*Absolutamente, no!*'

Gazing across the room at the elderly, frail man sitting in the wheelchair, Antonio Ramirez did his best to control his feelings of annoyance and irritation.

Not only was he very fond of his uncle Emilio, but he realised that he really must have patience with the old man who, since his last heart attack, had been forced to hand over the reins of the family business.

'Yes, I would agree that I face a difficult situation,' Antonio admitted, roughly brushing a hand through his thick, black curly hair. 'Particularly the urgent need to completely update our wine-making process. And, yes,' he added with a shrug of his broad shoulders, 'I would also agree that finding the millions to do so will not be easy. Although I believe I have solved that particular problem. But, nevertheless, your suggestion as to how I can best arrange my affairs is something which I find *totally* unacceptable!'

His uncle gave a heavy sigh. He really didn't understand young men nowadays, he told himself fretfully. None of them seemed in any hurry to get married, and Antonio—a handsome and extremely wealthy man, who'd left a whole host of glamorous girlfriends behind him in Madrid—was clearly no exception. But his nephew was now thirty-four, and it was clearly time he found himself a nice, sensible, financially well-endowed young girl and settled down.

'The engagement between myself and your late aunt was arranged by my parents. Although it may have been a marriage of convenience—bringing together two old families in the wine trade—it proved to be a very happy one. Even though, most unfortunately, we didn't have any children,' he pointed out querulously.

'Yes, I know, Uncle. And I do understand that you have my best interests at heart.'

'Well, I hope you've got enough sense not to get involved with Carlotta,' the older man muttered. 'That cousin of yours might be a good-looking girl but she's likely to cause you nothing but trouble!' he added, before realising from the blank, shuttered expression on his nephew's face that he'd gone too far.

'Thank you for your kind advice,' Antonio drawled icily. 'However, I must tell you that, strange as it may seem, I'm perfectly capable of running my private life without your assistance.'

'Yes, well...' His uncle shrugged. 'I may have been a bit out of order...'

Antonio gave a snort of grim laughter. 'You most certainly were! Especially since the idea of finding myself a rich wife is definitely *not* on my list of priorities just at the moment.'

'But, all the same, I do wish that...'

'Quite frankly, I'm far more interested in obtaining new contracts,' Antonio said, firmly changing the subject. 'Particularly in supplying our own brand of sherry to supermarkets in France, Germany and Italy. I also have high hopes of attracting some new business in North America,' he added, before quickly glancing down at his watch. 'Which is why I really must get back to work. I'm leaving tomorrow for a quick business trip around Europe,' he said, rising to his feet and walking towards the door.

'Unfortunately I can only afford to be away from the office for a week. But if I can manage to clinch those deals it will at least give us a breathing space. And also enable me to do some serious financial planning for the future.'

'You've mentioned America. What about the supermarkets in Britain?'

With his hand on the doorknob, Antonio paused, before turning slowly around, his dark eyebrows drawn together in a frown.

'I hadn't intended visiting London on this trip. But it now looks as if I may have to. I'm becoming increasingly worried about a large shipment of some of our very best wines which was dispatched to Brandon's of Pall Mall, in England, well over a month ago.'

'What's the problem?'

'I'm still not sure,' the younger man admitted with a slight shrug. 'For some reason, it appears to have gone missing. Needless to say I've been on the phone for the last two days, trying to track it down. But with absolutely no success so far.'

'Surely a consignment that large shouldn't be too hard to find?'

'Which is *precisely* what I have been telling those English wine merchants!' Antonio gave a short bark of sardonic laughter. 'I know Sir Robert Brandon is an old friend of yours, Uncle, but I have to say that it looks as though his methods of doing business are still firmly rooted in the nineteenth century!'

'You may regard Sir Robert and myself as ancient

dinosaurs,' his uncle retorted, 'but if you *do* go to
England it might be worth talking over your problems
with him. He is, after all, one of the cleverest businessmen in the wine trade.'

'Hmm…I'll think about it,' Antonio said as he
turned to open the door, not overly impressed with the
idea of picking the brains of his uncle's old friend.

'In the meantime—take care of yourself, Uncle. I
should be back in my office by next Monday,' he
added with a smile, before leaving the room.

Striding swiftly down the corridor towards the front
door of his uncle's house, Antonio could only feel
sorry for the elderly and infirm man, now confined to
a wheelchair.

However, the brutal facts of life were that if only
his uncle had resigned his position as head of the company immediately after becoming aware of his bad
heart condition the family business would not now be
in such a mess. Unfortunately the old man had refused
to listen to his doctor's advice, continuing to run the
business his own way and only finally relinquishing
control when forced to do so, after his last heart attack.

Which had meant that, instead of being able to make
long-term plans for taking over the family business,
Antonio had been forced to immediately abandon his
highly lucrative career as an international tax lawyer
in Madrid. And on his return home to Jerez he'd been
faced with some fairly major problems.

The most important of which was the urgent need
to bring modern organisation and technique into every
corner of the business, Antonio told himself grimly as
he left the house, running down the steps and across
to where his sports car was parked, beneath the shade
of some olive trees.

The extensive Ramirez family vineyards might produce some of the finest and most sought-after wines in the Spanish sherry trade, but his uncle had clearly never even heard of computers or the Internet. And there was virtually nothing in the way of records since his uncle had believed in handling as little paperwork as possible.

In fact, Antonio mused, drumming his fingers on the driving wheel of his car for a moment before switching on the engine, the meeting with his bankers this afternoon should, with any luck, help to solve most of his problems. Because the sooner he could start completely overhauling the family business the better!

Turning around his wheelchair, and gazing out through the open window as his nephew's black Porsche disappeared down the road in a cloud of dust, Emilio sat buried in thought for some time.

He was well aware of just how difficult it must have been for Antonio to give up his highly successful career. Not that the younger man had ever complained, of course. But it must have been a wrench to be forced to suddenly abandon his friends, colleagues and that glamorous apartment in Madrid simply because he was the only one in the family capable of running the business.

He clearly had no way of lightening Antonio's heavy burden, of course. But maybe...maybe there *was* something he could do about the financial problems facing his nephew...

While he might be stuck in this damned wheelchair there was still life in the old dog yet, Emilio told himself with a chuckle, before spinning around to pick up the phone on his desk.

'*Sí...*' he said as his call was answered at the other end of the line. '*Señor Don Roberto...por favor...*'

At approximately the same time, although many hundreds of miles away, Georgina Brandon was muttering furiously under her breath as she slammed down the phone.

She'd never got on with the manager of the company's headquarters at Pall Mall in London. And it was *just* like the slimy two-faced man to try and blame Gina and her staff for his own shortcomings.

Besides, exactly why he seemed to think such a very large, valuable consignment of top-class sherry would have been sent to the Ipswich branch office, here in Suffolk, she had absolutely no idea. Surely it was far more likely to be found at their other warehouse, in Bristol? Or most probably tucked away in the vast dusty cellars in Pall Mall.

But the loss of such a valuable shipment seemed the very least of her worries at the moment. Because— while she might enjoy hearing that the head of the world-famous Bodega Ramirez had well and truly chewed the ear off that creep in London—she'd been utterly devastated to learn exactly *who* was now the new Chairman and Managing Director of the Ramirez company.

'*Antonio? Antonio Ramirez?*' she'd gasped down the phone, just a few moments ago.

'Yeah. Surely you must have heard that he'd taken over the business from his old uncle Emilio?'

'No...no, I didn't know...' she'd muttered, her trembling hands almost dropping the phone as she'd tried to get her head around this startling and highly alarming piece of information.

'Well, well! Fancy clever Miss Georgina Brandon not being up with the latest news in the wine trade! I expect that's what comes of being stuck out in the boondocks of Suffolk,' the London manager had added with a slight laugh.

Feeling far too shattered to even try and cut the awful man down to size, she'd remained silent as he'd admitted that her grandfather was not at all happy about the situation.

'With Antonio Ramirez well and truly on the war-path, Sir Robert says that we've *got* to find that shipment, as fast as possible. Apparently the guy is a lawyer. And you know what they're like—never happier than when suing the socks off rich companies like your grandpa's! So, you'd better go through all the bills of lading with a fine-tooth comb. Or it could be *you* for the high jump,' he'd added with relish, before putting down the phone.

Still feeling stunned by the news of Antonio's direct involvement in his family's huge wine-making business, Gina took a deep breath.

It was no good sitting here at her desk in a complete daze, feeling as if she'd been suddenly hit very hard by a blow to the solar plexus, she told herself, brushing a shaky hand through her long, pale blond hair. She was really going to have to pull herself together— and try to get a firm grip on the situation.

After all…it was eight years since she'd seen hide or hair of the man with whom she'd fallen so desperately in love. But she'd been only eighteen at the time, for heaven's sake. And young girls were always falling in and out of love, with the *most* unsuitable men. It happened all the time. Besides, she'd had lots of boyfriends since then. And if none of them had ever caused the slightest dent in her heart? Well, she had plenty of time in hand before she needed to start worrying about finding Mr Right!

As branch manager of a large wine merchant's business she was used to dealing with the various fine sherries bearing the Bodega Ramirez label. So why get in such a panic just because this was the first time she'd heard any mention of Antonio's name?

What was more…if she'd ever stopped to think about it she ought to have known that sooner or later he was bound to succeed his uncle in the business. Just as she was due, eventually, to take over her grandfather's large, prestigious business.

Founded in 1791 by her ancestor, Captain James Brandon—who, after retiring from the navy and marrying a rich Spanish widow, had begun importing and blending high-quality sherry and wine from her family's vineyards near Cadiz—Brandon's of Pall Mall was now one of the oldest and most successful wine merchants in the country. Moreover, the ever-increasing value of the property owned by the family, particularly the large buildings situated in such an expensive area of London, was now enormous.

Handed down over the generations from father to son, the chain had been cruelly broken with the tragically early death of her parents in a car accident, when Gina had been only a little girl. Since her father had been an only child, she'd been raised by her grandparents, always knowing that she was the sole heiress to the family business.

Unfortunately, her increasingly desperate prayers each night—that her dear grandfather would remain at the helm for many years to come—were looking increasingly unlikely to be answered. He'd never really

recovered from the death of her beloved grandmother,
five years ago, and appeared to be growing more frail
in body, if not in spirit, with each passing day. And
she dreaded the prospect of having to take over the
running of the business in the near future.

On the other hand, her grandfather had certainly
done all he could to give her a good grounding in the
wine trade. He'd been pleased when she had devel-
oped a good 'nose' and palate, and delighted when
she'd passed the necessary exams to become a Master
of Wine. And now, with her recent appointment as
manager of the firm's Ipswich shop and warehouse,
she was in the process of gaining valuable business
experience.

But there was no getting away from the fact that
she *was* only twenty-six. And there was a world of
difference between running a small branch and managing a large international corporation.

However, all that lay in the future. In the meantime
she had to do her best to try and forget her past, very
brief relationship with Antonio Ramirez—and start
looking for his missing wine shipment!

But as it turned out that was easier said than done.

Four days later, and despite an exhaustive search of
the shop, warehouse and old cellars, Gina still hadn't
found any trace of the Spanish consignment. Moreover, having checked and double-checked the current
bills of lading, she'd drawn a complete blank there, as
well. So, wherever the missing shipment had got to, it
definitely wasn't in Suffolk!

Unfortunately, it seemed that the news about
Antonio Ramirez had prompted the return of that utterly hideous dream...the dreadful nightmare which
had repeatedly plagued her late teens and made her

life a misery for such a long time. For the past few days she'd found herself waking up after a disturbed, restless sleep, drenched in perspiration and trembling with deep shame and embarrassment.

Goodness knows, she'd done her best to bury those unhappy memories of when she'd obviously been far too young and innocent to understand the harsh realities of life. Which made it all the more maddening now to discover that Antonio's dark, highly dangerous figure had only been lurking just out of sight—hidden for the past eight years, somewhere within her subconscious, so that merely the mention of his name had brought him—and total recollection of that time in her life—sharply back to the surface of her mind once again.

Which was utterly daft! She'd got over him years ago. To let herself get into such a state was totally *pathetic*, Gina railed at herself angrily. But, although talking sternly to herself hadn't yet solved the problem, she knew that sooner or later the dreams would stop, and she could get back to her usual, mentally well-adjusted way of life.

All of which was sensible advice, Gina was telling herself firmly, late on Thursday morning, when the phone on her desk gave a sharp ring.

'Hi, Grandpa... Yes, yes, everything's fine,' she quickly assured the old man. 'No, I'm sorry. There's no trace of that shipment. I've been through every scrap of paperwork here in the office, and I can't find anything at all.'

'I'm afraid that's irrelevant now, since a representative of the Spanish firm is insisting on checking the stock in the warehouse,' Sir Robert Brandon's thin, reedy voice informed her.

'Well—that's a total waste of time,' she retorted. 'I *know* we haven't got it. I mean, we could hardly miss a shipment of that size, could we?'

'Nevertheless, I have Antonio Ramirez sitting in my outer office, here in London...'

'*What?*'

'...and I expect him to be with you either late in the afternoon or early this evening.'

'But...but...the office will be closed by then!' she retorted breathlessly, her knuckles whitening as she tightly gripped the phone. 'I mean, what's the point of him coming all the way up here and...and not being able to look for his beastly wine?'

'Really, Gina!' her grandfather protested. 'What on earth has come over you? I sincerely hope that I can rely on you to treat Don Antonio with every courtesy?'

'Yes...yes, of course. I'm sorry,' she mumbled helplessly, feeling totally stunned and somehow unable to stop herself trembling, as if in the grip of a raging fever.

'Oh, Lord! I've just realised...' she added hurriedly. 'If he's going to be arriving *that* late I'd better book him into one of the local country house hotels. Maybe Hintlesham Hall? The food is really excellent, and...'

'My dear girl—what *is* wrong with you?' Sir Robert Brandon retorted tetchily. 'For generations we've had a long-standing trading partnership with his company. And his uncle is, of course, an old friend of mine. Which is why I've already told Don Antonio that we wouldn't dream of him staying anywhere other than in our own home.'

'Our own home...?' she echoed vacantly, her numbed brain clearly not functioning on all cylinders.

'And I'm quite sure that I can rely on you to see

that he is well looked after,' her grandfather told her firmly, before terminating the call.

'Oh, my God...oh, my God... What in the hell am I going to do?' Gina found herself muttering, before jumping to her feet and striding rapidly up and down her office as she realised that matters were rapidly going from bad to far, *far* worse!

How *could* she have forgotten that she'd agreed to give the housekeeper and her husband a long weekend off, to visit their daughter in Wales? And, glancing down at her watch, she realised that they would have already left the house and be well on their way by now.

'For heaven's sake—calm down,' she said, forcing herself to stand still and take some deep breaths to steady her nerves.

It was a large old house, with many guest rooms, and she was *perfectly* capable of coping with Antonio on her own. After all, she was no longer a silly young girl, and was quite used to entertaining business guests. Besides, it was years since she'd set eyes on the man. Why, he could be married, with a whole host of children by now. Anyway, hadn't Grandpa said that Antonio wouldn't be arriving until this evening?

So...if she booked a table for dinner in a good local restaurant—making absolutely certain that *all* conversation was kept *firmly* to business matters—she shouldn't have too much of a problem. Then, when Antonio discovered that his missing shipment of wine definitely *wasn't* here, he'd obviously be off, back to wherever he'd come from, by midday tomorrow at the latest.

All the same...there was no point in sitting here in the office, feeling as though she was going to be sick any moment. In fact, the sooner she went home and checked that the beds were made up in the guest bedrooms the better.

While still feeling coiled up tight like an overwound clock spring, Gina could almost physically feel herself beginning to relax slightly as she drove her small Mazda sports car down the long drive, lined with ancient oak trees, to Bradgate Manor.

She'd always loved the large old Tudor mansion, which had been the country home of the Brandon family since the days of Queen Victoria—when it had been acquired by her great-great-grandfather for his young wife, who had been born and raised in Suffolk. And it was, of the course, one of the reasons why Gina had jumped at the opportunity of working in the local Ipswich office.

Who wouldn't prefer living deep in the country when compared to life in the crowded, dusty streets of London? Gina asked herself as she parked her car in the garage next to the stable block and walked slowly back towards the house. And especially on a lovely sunny day in early June, with no sound to disturb the peace other than the faint cooing of wood pigeons from a nearby clump of trees and the distant hum of a tractor in one of the fields.

Having checked that everything was in order, and deciding to place Antonio in a guest suite as far away from her own bedroom as possible, Gina found herself wandering restlessly through the empty house. In fact, she was feeling so tense and strained that she couldn't seem to keep still for more than a few seconds.

Firmly reminding herself that there was no reason why Antonio should recall the time when a young, gauche teenager had made such an utter fool of herself wasn't much use, either. Because, try as she might, she couldn't seem to banish from her mind's eye a vision of the dangerously exciting figure of Antonio Ramirez.

With his head of curly hair the colour of raven's wings—either worn loose, curling over his collar at the back of his neck, or wet-combed tightly to his head, after a shower—and the deeply disturbing, wicked glint in those large, gleaming dark eyes, heavily fringed with long black eyelashes, he'd been devastatingly attractive!

So it was no wonder, she told herself, that an impressionable young girl, fresh out of school, had immediately fallen head over heels in love with the most strikingly handsome man she'd ever seen. Who also happened to be the brother of her best friend, with whom she'd been staying during that Easter holiday all those years ago.

And Gina clearly hadn't been the only one to be so affected by the twenty-six-year-old man's aura of strong masculinity and rampant sex appeal. Just about every female in the large, extended Spanish family between the ages of nine and ninety had seemed to regard Antonio in exactly the same light.

'Just look at them!' Roxana had laughed. 'They're all over my brother, like a rash. *Estúpidas…no?*'

And she'd been the most *stupid* of all! Gina recalled grimly. Then she became furious with herself for getting in such a state about an episode—however shameful and embarrassing—which had happened so very long ago. Then she brought herself up with a start. This simply would *not* do! It was utterly *ridiculous* to keep on pacing up and down, getting more and more nervous with every passing minute, while waiting for the damned man to turn up. In fact, what she needed was some fresh air and exercise. So, the most sensible decision would be to get changed and take her horse out for a good hard gallop.

That would *definitely* blow the dusty cobwebs of memory from her mind, she told herself firmly, spinning around on her heels and running up the wide, old oak staircase towards her bedroom.

Antonio's lips tightened with annoyance as, for what seemed the hundredth time, he quickly stamped on the brake.

Having to drive a strange car on the wrong side of the road was bad enough. But the amount of traffic on this heavily congested route leading out of London was proving enough to try the patience of a saint.

However, taking into account the possible loss of his wine, *and* that quite extraordinary meeting with old Sir Robert Brandon, he told himself grimly, it now looked as if he'd made a *very* bad mistake by including this quick trip to Britain in his tight schedule.

'I'm so sorry, my boy,' Sir Robert Brandon had told him earlier today. 'It looks as if that shipment of yours has been misdirected to our branch at Ipswich, in Suffolk. I'll put my staff on to tracking it down straight away.'

Unfortunately, Sir Robert's idea of 'straight away' seemed to mean that it would take at least two weeks to sort out the problem.

'*Two weeks!*' Antonio had exclaimed in horror. 'But I hadn't planned to spend more than a day or two in England.'

However, after some discussion, he'd reluctantly agreed that his best and possibly only option was to visit Brandon's office and large warehouse at Ipswich, in Suffolk.

'It isn't a long drive,' Sir Robert had assured him. 'So why not allow me to show you around the cellars here, in Pall Mall, hmm? We have some very old cases of vintage wines which I think you might find interesting.'

Since the two families had been trading closely together for well over a hundred and fifty years, it had seemed discourteous to refuse the invitation. And that, as he now acknowledged grimly, had proved to be a major error on his part. Because after the tour of the wine cellars he'd found himself being pressured into joining Sir Robert for lunch.

'No…no, I can't possibly let you go without giving you something to eat,' the old man had insisted. 'And I've been looking forward to hearing all about my old friend Emilio. I was really so very sorry to hear about your uncle's illness.'

Finding himself boxed into a corner, Antonio hadn't seen that he'd had any choice but to accept the invitation. And with Sir Robert's servants moving like snails around the huge dining room of the large, private house in Pall Mall—taking hours to serve a very long, ridiculously grand meal—it had gradually become clear that he hadn't a hope of reaching Brandon's office in Suffolk before it had closed for the day.

If he'd had any sense, he *should* have written off that valuable consignment of sherry—high-tailing it back to Spain as quickly as possible. In fact, he *had* nearly called the whole thing off when Sir Robert had casually let fall the information that his granddaughter was currently managing the branch office in Ipswich.

'Gina's a clever girl,' the old man had continued. 'Only relation of mine still alive. So it seems a good way of giving her some experience of running things, before she takes over the business when I'm gone.'

Which was the first intimation he'd had that this trip to England might *definitely* prove to be a major mistake, Antonio told himself edgily, not at all sure how he felt about finding himself suddenly pitch-forked into dealing with a girl whom he hadn't seen for eight years.

And the subsequent conversation about the elderly man's frail health certainly hadn't improved matters either.

Swearing under his breath, Antonio drummed his fingers irritably on the driving wheel, trying to think what he was going to do about what appeared to be an increasingly tricky situation.

Because, of course, he had no problem recalling Gina Brandon, or the events of that weekend all those years ago when his family and their guests had attended the spring fiesta in Seville.

He hadn't forgotten how they'd avoided the rest of the party, determined to spend the day together. Nor her desperate terror as she'd tried to control a frisky young horse, when she'd clearly had neither the skills nor the experience to do so. Or the young girl's shy, enchanting smile and the long, pale blond hair swirling enticingly about her slim body as they'd become caught up in the hot-blooded, fiery Sevillanas—the traditional dance of Andalusia.

And then, surprising in its clarity, he suddenly recalled that ride in the early hours of the morning, through the empty and deserted streets of Seville. The ghostly sound of the horses' hooves over the cobbles.

And the moonlight, flooding in through the carriage window, which had thrown dark, mysterious shadows over the high cheekbones of the girl's heart-shaped face, causing her to look far older than her years. Which had been the only excuse he could find when recollecting with bitter shame his subsequent behaviour.

Forget it! That was all a *very* long time ago, he reminded himself grimly. In fact, there was every chance that she, at least, would have completely forgotten all about the unfortunate episode.

In any case, he had every intention of confining all conversation to the subject of business. Or that of the wine trade. And first thing tomorrow morning he'd locate his missing shipment and fly back to Spain—as quickly as possible.

Satisfied now that he'd come to a decision, Antonio realised, after a quick glance at the map, that he was nearing his destination. And only a few minutes later he caught sight of a large pair of wrought-iron gates bearing a sign: Bradgate Manor.

Travelling slowly down the long winding driveway, edged by tall oak trees, Antonio eventually brought his vehicle to a halt outside the front door of a large house.

Stepping out of the car, he stretched his tall, rangy body, clothed in a short-sleeved, open-necked black shirt and black trousers, before turning to gaze at the classical Tudor building.

The large diamond-paned windows were sparkling in the late-afternoon sun, which also cast long shadows over the old brickwork and heavy oak beams, the wide porch covered with rambling roses in shades of red and pink.

It seemed incredibly still and quiet as he made his way to the front door. In fact, other than the noise of his shoes crunching over the gravel, he could hear nothing except the rustle of a light breeze through the leaves of nearby trees.

Slightly surprised to find the front door wide open, Antonio rang the bell several times without gaining any response. However, after hesitating for some moments, he stepped inside, feeling slightly foolish as he called out to the unseen occupants. But, other than the sound of his own voice echoing in the large oak-beamed hall, the large house remained totally silent.

Perplexed, he walked slowly across the grey flag-stones towards a large door—which was also wide open—on the far side of the hall. This, as he discovered, opened out on to stone steps leading down to a wide terrace running the length of the house. Standing on the steps, he had an excellent view of the wide green lawn and its surrounding parkland.

Beginning to wonder if he had somehow wandered into an earthbound version of the *Marie Celeste*, Antonio suddenly caught sight of a horse and rider, galloping swiftly across the park towards the house.

Raising a hand to shield his eyes from the sun, now lying low in the sky as it slipped down over the horizon, he gradually realised two salient facts. Not only was the horse a huge, strong animal, but it gave every appearance of having the bit firmly between its teeth and bolting out of control. While the rider—clearly a female, if that long blonde hair was anything to go by—looked as if she was in trouble. In fact, as far as he could see, she seemed to be clinging helplessly to the horse's mane.

Without another moment's thought, Antonio ran

down the stone steps and raced across the lawn, before quickly vaulting over the wooden fence edging the park. Realising that he must try and stop the horse from attempting to jump the fence—with possibly grave consequences for its rider—he ran with arms outstretched towards the large animal.

The next few, brief seconds seemed to pass by in slow motion, as Antonio's action appeared to disconcert the huge beast. Thundering to a halt, it reared up before the strange man, its eyes rolling wildly, thick specks of white foam billowing from its mouth.

Leaping up to catch hold of the reins, and hanging on to them for dear life as the horse reared up again, its huge hooves beating in the air, he gradually managed to bring the animal under control. And it was only when he was murmuring soothing words, and gently stroking the horse's neck, that he had the opportunity to pay some attention to its rider.

Her chest heaving as she fought to catch her breath, she raised a hand to brush the long, tangled cloud of pale blonde hair from her face. And then, her blue eyes widening with shock and confusion, he could almost see the blood visibly draining from her pale cheeks.

'*Hola*, Gina!' he drawled, smiling up at the girl who appeared to be totally dumbfounded by his sudden appearance, stunned into silence and continuing to stare down at him as if he was a ghost.

'It looks as if you are still having problems with horses—just as you did all those years ago in Seville!' he laughed, keeping a firm grip on the reins with one hand, while putting out the other to help her dismount.

'So…it seems that I must come to your rescue—yet again! *No*…?'

CHAPTER TWO

'WHAT do you think you're doing?' Gina demanded angrily, when she was at last able to catch her breath.

'My dear Gina...what does it look as if I'm doing?' He grinned sardonically up at her. 'Surely I am—as you would say in England—rescuing a damsel in distress?'

'What?' She frowned down at him, not having a clue what he was talking about.

'Your horse was clearly out of control,' he pointed out, with a shrug of his broad shoulders. 'And, since you also appeared to be in some trouble, I naturally assumed...'

'Nonsense!' she snapped, leaning forward to give her horse a pat on the neck. 'There was absolutely no need to give poor Pegasus such a fright. And I certainly was *not* in trouble,' she added grimly, tightening her grip on the thin leather reins and giving them a quick jerk.

Desperately longing to be able to dig her heels into lazy old Pegasus, and get the hell out of this highly embarrassing situation, Gina realised that she was well and truly stuck. Now that he was so near his stable, her beastly horse wasn't likely to budge an inch. And with Antonio continuing to grin sardonically up at her—while still maintaining his iron grip on the reins—there was clearly nothing she could do.

'Nevertheless, this animal appeared to be clearly terrified, and bolting out of control,' Antonio pointed

27

out in a maddening, condescending tone of voice. 'Which is precisely why, my dear Gina, I quickly realised that I must come to your rescue. Yet again!' he added with a low rumble of laughter.

'Hah! That's all you know!' she ground out furiously, her palms itching to smack that superior smile off his handsome face.

Quickly slipping one of her black leather boots out of its stirrup, she swung her leg up over the saddle and jumped lightly down on to the ground beside him.

And that, Gina realised almost immediately, had been a bad, *bad* mistake.

For one thing, she had immediately lost the advantage of height which she'd had when perched on her horse's back. And although at five foot ten inches she was normally regarded as being a tall woman, she now found herself having to look up at the man standing beside her.

And besides…well, now that she was standing so close to him, she could almost feel the tough, physical aura, the dramatic sense of power and overwhelming masculine sexuality, which had always seemed to positively ooze from every pore of Antonio's tall, dynamic figure.

Nothing has changed, she told herself with a sinking heart. How could life be so unfair? Surely after all this time he could at least have done her the great favour of becoming disgustingly fat…or bald…or as ugly as sin…

Unfortunately, as much as it might hurt her to admit the truth, it seemed as if the passage of time had hardly touched the rotten man.

In fact, with that short-sleeved black shirt emphasising his broad shoulders, and those trousers posi-

tively hugging his slim waist and hips, he was clearly
in great shape. Although his face now seemed slightly
thinner than she remembered—throwing into relief his
high cheekbones, and giving him a more hawk-like
expression—he was still the same diabolically attractive man she'd known all those years ago.

*Come on! Get a grip on the situation. You've got
to pull yourself together—and fast!* she yelled silently
at her inner self, who was clearly going weak at the
knees in response to his overwhelming sex appeal. Not
to mention the soft, caressing effect his Spanish accent
was having on her trembling body.

How *could* she be so stupid, for heaven's sake? This
man had always been Trouble with a capital *T*, as far
as she was concerned. And she'd be an idiot not to
keep that thought *firmly* at the very front of her mind!

'If you must know…far from bolting, as you put it,
greedy old Pegasus was just galloping back to his stable—looking forward to a fresh bag of hay!' she told
Antonio through gritted teeth.

'He *always* does that when we turn for home after
being out for a ride,' she added, brushing the long fair
hair from her face as she raised her chin defiantly towards him. 'And I happen to enjoy the gallop home
every bit as much as he does!'

'Ah…'

'So, you see…I most certainly did not need rescuing
by you, *señor*!'

'"*Señor*"…?' he murmured dryly, and her cheeks
flushed as she registered the cool, ironic tone in his
deep voice. 'Ah, Gina! Surely I was once "Antonio"
to you…?'

'Yes…well…that was a very long time ago,' she
muttered, bitterly aware of the breathless, husky note

in her own voice and the hot tide of crimson now sweeping up over her pale complexion. 'I...er...I'm a completely different person nowadays.'

'Umm...yes, I can see that you most certainly are!' he drawled, his dark eyes fringed with long, thick lashes gleaming with sardonic amusement as he viewed the tall, slender figure standing beside him.

With her long, ash-blonde hair flowing down well past her shoulders, it was obvious to Antonio that the young girl whom he'd once known had now matured into a beautiful woman. Her pale alabaster skin, fine bone structure and high forehead over hauntingly vivid sapphire-blue eyes all combined to give her a faintly medieval appearance. Just the sort of looks, in fact, which would have recommended her to artists such as Leonardo da Vinci and Michelangelo.

Regrettably, however, his rather more down-to-earth, basic instincts were irrepressibly drawn to her high, firm breasts, and the slim waist and hips emphasised by those close-fitting jodhpurs.

Why was it, he found himself wondering idly, that the sight of a woman dressed in pale-coloured, skin-tight riding breeches and high, shiny black boots appeared to be quite so erotic?

However, he quickly realised, only a second or two later, that Miss Gina Brandon did not seem to appreciate him viewing her with such close interest. Especially if the sight of the angry glint in her large blue eyes, and those soft lips now drawn into a hard, tight line of annoyance was anything to go by!

Damned cheek! Gina gritted her teeth, fuming with resentment.

Having been a bag of nerves all afternoon and feeling sick with apprehension about the sudden reap-

pearance of Antonio in her life, Gina was now almost
grateful for the tide of fury surging through her veins.
Besides, rage and anger *had* to be much safer emotions
than the highly dangerous siren call of Antonio's over-
whelmingly sensual appeal, to which she'd found herself so weakly responding earlier.

Struggling to overcome yet another urgent desire to
give that handsome tanned face a good, hard slap, she
forced herself to take a deep breath.

'I think we've stood out here in the park quite long
enough—don't you?' she said as coolly as she could,
before stalking past Antonio towards the wooden fence
and swinging open a five-barred gate.

Since he'd been so determined, earlier, to hang on
to Pegasus's reins, he could damn well be useful and
lead the horse back to its manger, she thought defiantly, simply not caring if she was being a lousy hostess as she strode ahead of him towards the stable
block.

However, by the time that Pegasus was unsaddled,
and safely bedded down in his stable, Gina had managed to get herself back on an even keel. Helped, it
must be said, by the completely unexpected, matter-
of-fact way in which Antonio, without needing to be
asked, had automatically brushed down the large animal while she'd filled nets with fresh hay, for both
Pegasus and the elderly mare whom she kept as his
stable companion.

'Would you care for a pot of tea?' Gina asked as
she bolted the door of the stables before leading the
way towards the house. 'Or maybe...' She glanced
down at her watch as they entered the hall, surprised
to see that it was almost six o'clock. 'Maybe you'd
prefer a drink?'

While Antonio, who'd never understood the fondness of the English for their traditional cup of tea, was agreeing that a drink would be welcome, Gina caught sight of herself in a large mirror on the wall.

It was all she could do not to groan out loud with dismay. It was deeply galling to realise that she'd spent the last half-hour looking such a fright. Because it must have been in the stable that she'd picked up those bits of straw in her hair, and the large smear of dust on her face.

Just as she was wondering if she could leave Antonio to twiddle his thumbs, while she rushed upstairs and tried to make herself look more presentable, she was startled to see the reflection of his tanned, handsome face appearing beside her.

'Oh, Lord—what a mess!' she muttered, giving him a fleeting, nervous smile in the mirror as she quickly tried to brush the dust from her cheek.

'No problema...' he murmured, standing close behind her tense figure and calmly plucking the long, thin pieces of straw from her tangled locks.

Unable to prevent an involuntary slight shiver at the touch of his warm fingers brushing against her skin, Gina was surprised to find herself meekly allowing him to turn her around. And, even more astonishingly, waiting patiently while he took a clean handkerchief from his pocket and proceeded to slowly brush the dust from her cheek.

'That's much better,' he said, taking a step back and allowing his gaze to roam slowly, once more, over her full breasts and slim-waisted figure.

'Oh, yes...you've *definitely* grown up since we last met, Gina,' he drawled, the sardonic amusement in his voice suddenly setting her teeth on edge. 'And now we can maybe have that drink you mentioned?'

She was swept by a sudden, quick flash of furious self-disgust at having allowed herself to be cut down to size. And by *this* man, of all people, she told herself grimly, fed up to the back teeth at the alarming speed with which her emotions seemed to be violently swinging up and down from one minute to the next.

It was like…well, it was just like being on a roller-coaster, she told herself, before giving him a curt nod and stomping off across the hall. The sharp, staccato sound of her leather-soled boots on the hard grey flag-stones betrayed her momentary anger, and caused Antonio's lips to twitch with amusement as he followed her into a large kitchen.

'There's some beer and a bottle of wine in the fridge. However, if you'd prefer something stronger…?'

Having assured her that chilled white wine would be perfect, and after carrying the small tray outside on to the terrace, Antonio raised the question of why the house had appeared to be so deserted on his arrival.

'It wasn't too clever of me to leave all the doors open,' she admitted, sitting down on the long stone seat set against the side of the house and trying not to stare at his long, tanned fingers as they deftly removed the cork from the wine bottle.

'Although we usually do, if it's a hot afternoon like today,' she told him with a slight shrug, before adding carelessly, 'But I suppose I should have remembered that the Lamberts are away for a long weekend.'

Antonio raised a dark, quizzical eyebrow. 'The Lamberts…?'

Damn! Why didn't I keep my stupid mouth shut?
Gina asked herself irritably.

She was a grown woman, and quite sensible enough
to realise that while Antonio might well try and flirt
with her that was as far as he was likely to go. And,
let's face it, she told herself wryly, he was just the sort
of guy who automatically turned on the charm whenever in the presence of a female—whatever their age
might be.

However, she really didn't want him to get the
wrong idea. It was just possible that, having told him
she was alone in the house, he might think she was
expecting him to come on to her. So…it might be as
well to hit *that* nail hard on the head straight away.

'Yes, the housekeeper and her husband, Doris and
Ted Lambert, are away for the weekend,' Gina said as
he handed her a glass of wine. 'They've looked after
the house—and my grandfather—for the last twenty
years. Quite honestly,' she added with a quick grin, 'I
don't know what we'd do without them.'

'Ah, yes, I see.'

'However…Doris always lays on one of her friends
in the village to come in and clean when she's away.
And since her friend is apt to sing hymns at the top
of her voice, early in the morning, I've given you a
bedroom suite in the far wing of the house,' Gina told
him, adding casually, 'As far away from the main
block and the other bedrooms as possible.'

'I see. All is explained,' he murmured enigmati-
cally, leaving her to worry about whether she'd been
too obvious as he came over to sit down on the stone
bench beside her. 'But it must be a problem having
no cook in the kitchen?'

'Nonsense!' Gina laughed nervously, wishing that

he had chosen to sit on one of the comfortable garden chairs instead. Unfortunately, there was no getting away from the fact that she was finding the close proximity of this man distinctly disturbing.

'I'm perfectly capable of cooking a meal,' she told him briskly. 'Good wine and good food are natural partners. Which is why I spent a year doing a cordon bleu course in Paris, when I left school. However, since I didn't have much warning of your arrival today, I've booked a table for dinner at one of the local restaurants,' she added, before rising to her feet and suggesting that he might like to be shown to his room.

Luckily, the situation wasn't proving to be nearly so awkward as she had feared, Gina told herself some hours later, as she leaned back in her chair, gazing around the crowded restaurant.

In fact, he appeared to approve of her very plain, black silk sleeveless dress, and the simple row of pearls which had belonged to her mother. And apart from a slight altercation when Antonio had adamantly insisted on them leaving the house in *his* car—'I have never allowed myself to be driven by a woman—and I have *no* intention of doing so now!'—he was proving to be the perfect guest.

He'd also been charmed by the sight of the ivy-covered restaurant situated at the end of a narrow country lane, nodding with satisfaction when they'd been shown to a secluded table in the beautifully decorated dining room. Which clearly gave them some degree of privacy, and the opportunity of holding a conversation without being deafened by the chattering noise of the other diners.

'I'd forgotten that it can be quite so noisy at times,'

she'd murmured apologetically, but he'd brushed her
words aside.

'That, my dear Gina, is merely the sign of a good
restaurant,' he'd told her, before turning his attention
to the wine list.

Fortunately he'd approved of the wine list—always
a tricky point when taking those in the trade out to
dinner!—and there'd been some considerable discussion with the attentive head waiter over exactly what
to drink with their choice of cold watercress soup and
chicken in a tarragon sauce.

Not only had the wine and food proved to be delicious, but she'd found herself gradually relaxing and
enjoying Antonio's company: laughing at his wry,
amusing description of the total chaos he'd discovered
in the Bodega when taking over the reins of the family
company from his uncle Emilio. 'I'm not saying that
the invoices were still being written with a quill pen.'
He'd grinned. 'But the ancient telephone switchboard
had clearly not been changed since the days of
Alexander Graham Bell!'

And, of course, she'd been delighted to hear the up-
to-date news of her old friend—his younger sister,
Roxana, whom she'd met when the Spanish girl had
spent a year at school in London to brush up her
English.

Drawn together by the fact that they were both or-
phans—Roxana's parents having also been killed in a
car accident when she was only a small child—they'd
not only become firm friends, but had spent long hol-
idays at each other's homes. Which was precisely how
she'd first come to meet Antonio, Gina reminded herself, before quickly making a determined effort to banish the past from her mind.

'She was always an amusing girl, *no*?' Antonio had said with a broad smile, before explaining that his young sister, to the surprise of the whole family, had suddenly decided to take up a career in show business and was now appearing in one of the daily soap operas on Spanish television.

'Good heavens!' Gina had exclaimed, her smile widening when he'd informed her that those were *exactly* the same words used by his elderly grandmother on first seeing Roxana on TV. She'd been really pleased to hear that his old grandmother, Señora Ramirez, of whom she had fond memories, was still very much alive and ruling the roost at the family home in Jerez—where, it seemed, Antonio was also now based, since taking over the company.

Indeed, from what Antonio had said, it seemed as if he was going to have his work cut out, trying to drag the family wine business into the twenty-first century. And, thinking about some of the problems which he'd outlined, such as the need to make sure all his aged relatives continued receiving a reasonable income, Gina suddenly realised that it couldn't have been much fun suddenly finding himself pitchforked into taking on the family responsibilities.

'Do you have any regrets about having been forced to give up your career in the law?' she'd asked. 'The life of a wine maker in Jerez must be very different to that of a hot-shot lawyer in Madrid.'

'I always knew that I would have to, at some point in my life, take over the family business, but my uncle was always very much of an autocrat,' Antonio had said, with a shrug of his broad shoulders. 'Which was why I decided to carve out a career of my own, until such time as my uncle Emilio decided to hand over

the reins. And it would seem that you, too, are likely
to be faced with very much the same sort of situation,
if and when your grandfather decides to retire,' he'd
added with a smile.

However, she'd merely given a slight shrug of her
own, before determinedly changing the subject by asking him his opinion of last year's wines from the fa-
mous Rioja region in the north of Spain.

Despite doing her best to try and keep all conversation to their mutual business interest, Gina had found
it increasingly difficult to harden her heart against his
warm, obvious charm.

She must be careful, she warned herself now, as she
leaned back in her seat to allow the waiter to clear
away their plates. Not only did Antonio seem to have
bowled over the restaurant's staff with his engagingly
friendly smile, but *she* was also clearly vulnerable.
And she knew, only too well, just how this formidable
man's dark, almost irresistible attraction could affect
her fragile emotions.

So, keep it light...light and friendly, she lectured
herself sternly. Because, the last, the *very* last thing
she wanted was *any* discussion about their past relationship.

Although to be fair to Antonio, she reminded herself, by the time he was driving them back home to
Bradgate Manor, he'd made absolutely no reference to
what had happened between them years ago.

'It has been a very pleasant evening, Gina,' he said,
as he brought the car to a halt outside her home. He
got out of the car and came around to open the passenger door. 'Quite surprisingly so, in fact,' he added,
putting a hand on her arm as they walked towards the
front door.

'Oh…er…really?' she muttered breathlessly, in-
wardly cursing her fumbling fingers, which seemed all
over the place as she awkwardly tried to fit the key
into the lock.

'Here—let me do that for you,' he said, his lips
twitching with laughter, taking the keys from her hand
and swiftly unlocking the door.

'Yes…' he continued as they entered the hall. 'I
must admit to having felt some qualms about meeting
you again, after all these years. It might have been
just…well, shall we say that it might have been *just* a
little awkward?'

'I don't know what you mean,' she retorted, furious
with herself for sounding so pathetically feeble, but
not feeling capable of coping with this increasingly
difficult situation.

'Ah, Gina! Did you really forget all about me?' he
murmured, his tall figure standing close beside her
now, at the foot of the staircase. 'I am very sorry to
hear that I meant so little to you.'

Forget him? I should have been so lucky!

'No, well…the fact is…whatever happened…if
anything did happen…a long time ago…and I really
don't think…' she babbled incoherently, desperately
wishing that she could suddenly sink through a hole
in the floor and disappear safely from sight.

Unfortunately, while she had no trouble forming the
words in her head, she was managing to sound an
awful fool when trying to articulate them out loud.
And what seemed to be making the problem ten times
worse was the fact that he was now standing so close
to her.

'What I mean,' she said, pulling herself together
with some difficulty and attempting to sound a lot

more confident than she felt, 'is that whatever happened in the past is now—certainly as far as I'm concerned—dead and gone. To be truthful,' she added, with as much dignity as she could muster, 'I was a very young, silly girl at the time. And no one with any sense would wish to remember such a humiliating experience. So, I would be grateful if you would kindly *not* refer to the matter ever again.'

Antonio regarded her silently for a moment, before giving a brief shrug of his shoulders.

'I will, of course, respect your decision,' he murmured. 'However...I must tell you that I still have some very fond memories of that time in Spain.'

Taking hold of her hand, he lifted it slowly to his lips. 'Very fond memories, indeed,' he added, pressing his soft lips to her trembling fingers once again, before letting go of her hand and turning to walk away across the hall.

Gazing at the tall figure lithely mounting the staircase towards his room on the far side of the house, Gina found her mind in a complete turmoil. And even when lying in her own bed, later that night, wide awake and unable to seek refuge in sleep, she could still hear his words pounding through her brain.

Despite having tossed and turned restlessly throughout the night, Gina awoke the next morning feeling surprisingly bright and cheerful.

Which must be due to the fact that there'd been no return of that awful nightmare, she assured herself. Although, to be honest, having firmly told Antonio that she was *not* prepared to discuss the past, in any shape or form, had probably also contributed to her feeling of well-being.

Not to mention the important fact that he really

didn't seem to regard their previous relationship in quite the same embarrassing light as she did.

So it was not surprising that, being relieved of the burden which she'd carried for so long, over the eight past years, she should now be feeling quite euphoric. Besides, the sun was shining. It was a lovely, fresh June morning. And, having showered, washed and blow-dried her hair, before slipping on a short-sleeved white blouse and tucking it inside the waistband of her straight, navy blue linen skirt, Gina told herself that it was no wonder she felt remarkably cheerful.

Unfortunately, as happened so often in life, the happy frame of mind in which she'd greeted the new day was fast disappearing by the time she and Antonio returned to the office, after a brief lunch in a local pub.

After a promising start—with Antonio appearing downstairs promptly for breakfast that morning and confirming that he'd spent a comfortable night before driving them both in his car to the office—things had promptly begun to go downhill from then on.

With two of her staff away—one on holiday and the other nursing a sick husband—Gina had known that she was likely to be short-staffed. But when Antonio had commandeered another two workers—'I'm sorry, *querida*,' he'd said, almost idly running a finger down her soft cheek, 'but I really *must* locate that missing consignment'—she'd found herself being forced to work flat out all morning.

The situation had not been helped, it must be said, by the strange difficulty she had in concentrating on anything, his casual Spanish endearment and the touch of his finger on her face having left her feeling extraordinarily jumpy and strung up with nervous tension.

'I told both Grandpa and the manager at our office in Pall Mall that we really did *not* have that consignment of yours on our premises,' she told Antonio now, as they returned to the office after lunch. 'As you've seen for yourself, it simply isn't here.'

'You would appear to be quite correct,' he agreed with a heavy sigh. 'However, while there's no trace of the shipment in those bills of lading, I think that I must check through your warehouse and cellars myself, just to make certain that there's no possibility of a mistake.'

Gina shrugged her slim shoulders. 'I suppose that's sensible,' she commented. 'But I'm afraid you can't have those two young men who were helping you this morning. There's a whole mass of cases which need delivering around the town, and I can't afford to take them off duty and place them at your disposal.'

'Fair enough. However, there's no reason why you can't show me around the cellars, is there?'

'No, of course not,' she agreed, painfully aware of the considerable amount of work already piling up on her own desk. Still, it would be a bonus to prove—if only to that awful manager in London—that there'd been no mismanagement in her branch, she told herself, collecting the keys from a drawer in her desk before leading him through the large old warehouse and down into the underground cellars.

This definitely wasn't her favourite sort of place, Gina thought, glancing around the large, dark and dank cavernous space, located well below the level of the road above them.

With only a few shafts of daylight slanting in from

the small windows set high up on the wall, this place was definitely very spooky. And all those huge cobwebs didn't help, either! Glancing up at what seemed to be yards of dusty, tattered lace curtains hanging from the ceiling, she figured there must be a whole army of spiders spending their days spinning away like crazy. Ugh! Quite frankly, the sooner she was out of here, the happier she'd be!

'No...as far as I can see there is no trace of my missing shipment down here,' Antonio said, brushing the dust and cobwebs from his hands and looking about him as he approached her through an aisle of heavy cardboard cases. 'Although, you certainly seem to have some interesting old wines stored down here,' he added, coming to a halt beside her.

'Yes. I think that some of them have been here since my great-great-grandfather's day,' she muttered, suddenly feeling rather peculiar.

Maybe it had something to do with the strange tones and shades of light down here in the cellar. Or the feeling of being dwarfed beneath the large stone columns supporting the roof, way above their heads. But, while he hadn't said anything, and wasn't even touching her, the physical sensations which she'd always associated with Antonio whenever she was in close proximity to his tall figure had suddenly returned with a vengeance. Her pulse felt as if it was racing out of control, and she could feel a deep flush spreading over her skin—an extraordinary sensation of white heat surging through her body.

The huge, vaulted room seemed to be shrinking about them, their two still figures caught in a time warp—one in which she was feeling increasingly weak and light-headed. The strained silence seemed to last

for ever as she stared up into his gleaming dark eyes—
a silence beating loudly on her eardrums as her mind
was filled with disturbing, sensually erotic memories
of the last time she'd found herself clasped in his arms.

As he took another slow step towards her nervous,
trembling figure, she could feel her heart beginning to
pound like a heavy drum, the thudding against her ribs
producing a swift surge of adrenaline throughout her
body and leaving her breathless, as though she'd just
taken part in a hard-fought race.

Her mouth was suddenly feeling dry with a strange
mixture of fear and tension. However, as she uncon-
sciously moistened her lips with her tongue, he seemed
to stiffen, his low, tersely muttered oaths suddenly cutting into the claustrophobic and highly oppressive silence.

'Oh...um...just look at the time...I really must get
back to the office...' she gabbled, quickly spinning
around on her heels and almost running towards the
stairs leading out of the cellars, frantically anxious to
get back to the normal, prosaic light of day. And well
away from the highly disturbing Antonio Ramirez.

Walking swiftly towards her office, she almost
bumped into her secretary, coming down the corridor
towards her and brandishing a piece of paper in her
hand.

'I've just had a fax from our Bristol office, Miss
Brandon,' the girl said breathlessly, before raising her
eyes past Gina's shoulders as Antonio approached
them.

'They've found your missing shipment of wine in
Bristol, Señor Ramirez,' she told him with a wide,
beaming smile.

'Bueno.' He grinned, taking the paper from her

hands and quickly glancing down at the information it contained. 'This is very satisfactory,' he told the girl, giving her a warm smile of approval which clearly left her almost reeling with delight.

The man uses his charm like a weapon! Gina thought grimly, continuing on into her office and throwing herself down into the chair behind her desk in a thoroughly bad temper.

Yes, *of course* she was pleased that Antonio had at last found his precious shipment of wine. But, quite honestly, it was absolutely *disgusting* the way he only had to smile at a woman and she practically fell over backwards with excitement. Well! He needn't think that *she* was prepared to behave in such a stupid fashion!

No, indeed! a small inner voice pointed out with heavy sarcasm. *After all, now that Antonio has found his precious shipment of wine, you're going to be thrilled to bits to see the last of him—aren't you?*

Oh—shut up! she told herself impatiently, well aware that she was not looking forward to his departure. After all it had taken her ages to recover from her last meeting with this man. Now with her emotions all over the place she had a horrid feeling that it would be a long, *long* time before she got over this recent encounter.

Hey! Where's your pride, girl? she asked herself. There's no way you're going to let him guess just what a devastating effect he's having on you. Right?

Damn right! She agreed firmly, before standing up, nervously brushing down her skirt and preparing to face the world—and Antonio—with a confident and happy smile.

The discovery that the wine was safely tucked away

in the cellars in Bristol, and was being immediately transported down to Brandon's headquarters in Pall Mall, seemed to have acted as a tonic as far as the staff of the Ipswich branch were concerned. And certainly Antonio himself seemed remarkably content, humming cheerfully under his breath as, in the late afternoon, he drove her back to Bradgate Manor.

For her part, Gina didn't feel exactly like breaking into song. In fact, she was feeling highly depressed about the whole business. Although she was doing her best to keep that damned happy smile firmly pinned to her lips.

Still…she wouldn't have to keep up the façade for very long. Just as soon as he'd collected his luggage Antonio would undoubtedly be off back down to London, impatient to catch a flight back to Spain.

'Did you really spend a year doing a cookery course in Paris?' Antonio said, breaking the silence as he brought the car to a halt outside the house.

'Yes…yes I did,' she confirmed, wondering why he should be interested as they walked across the gravelled forecourt and up the steps to the front door.

'Excellent! So, you would have no problem in feeding a hungry man before he has to face the long journey back to London?'

'What?' She turned to gaze at him in surprise. 'I'm not sure I quite understand? Do you mean that you'd like to stay and…and have dinner with me tonight?'

'What a delightful idea! I am happy to accept your kind invitation.' He grinned, his amusement deepening as he caught the slight flicker of consternation in her startled blue eyes.

'If it's too much of an imposition, I will quite understand,' he murmured. 'I would hate to put you to any inconvenience. You have only to say the word, and...'

'Oh—shut up!' she muttered, well aware that he was laughing at her. 'Yes, of course you can stay and have dinner,' she added, making an effort to pull herself together as she led the way into the hall.

'It is certainly very pleasant to be sitting here, drinking an excellent glass of wine and admiring the view,' Antonio drawled some time later, leaning back against the warm brickwork of the house and stretching out his long legs. 'And doubly enjoyable with the prospect of sampling your culinary expertise, of course.'

'I wouldn't get *too* excited about that, if I were you,' she told him caustically, wondering what the heck she could come up with—and at virtually no notice. Apart from anything else—and recalling his long deliberations over the menu last night—she had a nasty feeling that Antonio's standards were more than likely to be extremely high.

And exactly *why* he wanted her to cook him a meal she had no idea. Surely he would want to get on the road as soon as possible?

But she hadn't any time to worry about that just at the moment. If she wanted to have a bath and change before hitting the kitchen it looked as if she'd have to get her skates on.

Later, as she lay in the bath, immersed in foam bubbles, Gina realised that she really couldn't stay here all day. Glancing over at her watch on the stool beside the tub, she realised that it was time she got herself downstairs to the kitchen. But, what the heck! It wouldn't do Antonio any harm to cool his heels for a while.

However, as she got out of the bath, wrapping a

thick, fluffy towel about her damp figure, there was only one really important question on her mind at that moment. What was she going to wear?

She'd thought of giving Antonio a boring one-course meal in the kitchen—which would serve him right for inviting himself to dinner! But, lying in the bath, she'd come up with another plan. Although she was beginning to wonder if it was really such a good idea, after all.

Regarding herself in a full-length mirror, some minutes later, she was pretty sure that it wasn't!

She'd wound her long hair up, securing it on top of her head with some antique tortoiseshell combs—which she hoped would make her look a whole lot more sophisticated. And there was nothing *actually* wrong with the dress, either. It was just that the knee-length dress of thin black crêpe, cut on the bias and clinging tightly to her full breasts and slim hips, left little to the imagination. And the low-cut, deep V of the bodice, held up by spaghetti-thin straps over her shoulders, would have caused her dear grandmother to scream out loud in horror!

Her initial impulse, when lying in the bath tonight—clearly *very* unworthy though it might have been—had been to show Antonio just what he'd turned down all those years ago. But now, as she stood in front of the mirror, she realised that it had been an utterly stupid idea.

For one thing it seemed such a childish response to the situation. And for another…well, she had to admit that he'd been an extremely pleasant guest, who'd even told her last night—although he'd probably been lying through his teeth—that he had nothing but happy memories of her.

Besides, she wasn't at all sure she could carry it off. Especially not in front of Antonio who, most unfortunately—and however much she might try to deny the fact, even to herself—still seemed to have the ability to make her feel most peculiar. Her stomach churned with a weird mixture of breathless excitement and a slightly nauseous feeling of nervous tension whenever she found herself anywhere near him.

Still…it was too late to change her mind now. And so, slipping on a pair of black high-heeled sandals and giving herself a quick spray of her new favourite perfume, she left her bedroom to go downstairs.

Comforting herself with the thought that, with any luck, she'd be able to slip quietly into the kitchen and put on her chef's apron—which would at least have the effect of making her look more respectable—Gina quickly discovered she was doomed to disappointment.

Moving swiftly down the old oak staircase, she had just taken her first step into the hall when she saw Antonio's tall figure coming in through the door leading out on to the terrace.

Damn! That's torn it! she told herself grimly. But it was obviously far too late for her to try and dash back upstairs.

And so, taking a deep breath and determinedly ignoring the hard lump of apprehension which seemed to be settling like a stone in her stomach, she walked calmly across the flagstones towards him.

CHAPTER THREE

WELL…all right, maybe Antonio hadn't *exactly* fainted with horror when first setting eyes on her in that dress. But he'd definitely stood gazing at her with a stunned expression for some seconds. Almost as if he'd been hit very hard on the back of his head by a large sandbag.

All in all, it had been a *very* satisfactory reaction! Certainly as far as she was concerned, Gina told herself with a grin, putting down her knife and sprinkling the chopped parsley onto a white sauce. In fact, when Antonio had closed his eyes for a moment, before taking another dazed look at the girl standing across the hall, she'd felt confident enough to give him a cool, sophisticated smile, before walking slowly past him into the kitchen.

What was that old saying? 'Revenge is a dish best served cold'? Well, she'd had to wait a very long time, of course. All the same, it looked as though the absolutely outrageous amount of money which she'd had to pay for this dress had *definitely* been worth every penny!

Having scraped the new potatoes and shelled fresh green peas from the kitchen garden, she was just chopping some more herbs when Antonio walked into the kitchen, carrying two glasses of wine.

He had clearly taken the opportunity to wash and change his clothes while she was having a bath and getting dressed; his hair was still damp from the shower, combed tightly to his head and curling up over his collar at the back.

'I am looking forward to dinner with some anticipation,' he announced with a grin, putting a glass down on the kitchen table beside her. 'In fact, I can't recall having a meal *à deux* where the lady concerned was not only beautiful but also a cordon bleu cook,' he added, removing his pale cream suede leather jacket and placing it on the back of a chair, before leaning casually against the large, old-fashioned kitchen dresser, smiling at her over his own glass of wine.

Oh, yeah? Gina thought, raising a sceptical eyebrow and giving him a slightly ironic smile, before tipping finely chopped shallots, basil and chives into a small bowl containing cream cheese.

That was a nice, flattering statement, of course, but who did Antonio think he was kidding? Because she was quite certain that this devastatingly attractive man would have *no* problem in obtaining, if he so wished, the culinary expertise of *any* amount of good-looking women.

Just look at the way he was affecting her, for heaven's sake!

Even one glance at the strong column of his throat, rising from the white open-necked shirt with its short sleeves displaying the deeply tanned skin of those strong, muscular arms, had been enough to set her pulse racing. And the sight of those beautifully tailored trousers, tightly clinging to his slim waist and hips, was enough to raise her blood pressure!

In fact, to be absolutely blunt, this man was clearly a health hazard as far as most of the female population was concerned. How she was supposed to concentrate on producing even a halfway decent meal when she was feeling so breathless and almost sick with nerves she hadn't the faintest idea.

Gazing at Gina as she moved deftly around the kitchen, Antonio wasn't sure whether to be pleased or disappointed to see that she was now wearing a thick white cotton apron. He'd certainly appreciated the sight of her in that ridiculously sexy dress.

However, he was intent on getting to know her better—and hadn't reached the age of thirty-four without acquiring some considerable experience of women. So, it might be as well if he did his best to ignore the flames of the obviously strong, sensual attraction which were almost visibly crackling between himself and Gina.

He had also noted, with some amusement, her faintly sardonic response to his compliment.

What a pity that he was having to fly back to Spain on Monday! The young girl he'd known some eight years ago had now clearly matured into a delightful, strong-minded and highly desirable woman.

'So, what are we going to eat tonight?' he asked.

'You didn't give me much notice. So it's going to be a case of pot luck, I'm afraid,' she told him with a slight shrug. 'I thought we'd start with fresh tomatoes, stuffed with cream cheese and herbs. And then, because the Grimsby Flyer called by yesterday...'

'The *what*?' He frowned in puzzlement.

'It's a van which zips around this part of East Anglia selling freshly caught fish from door to door,' she explained, before adding that, while fillets of cod in parsley sauce might sound a bit boring, she reckoned that really fresh cod was a highly underrated fish.

'As for pudding...' she continued. 'How do you feel about gooseberry fool?'

He shrugged. 'I have no idea. In fact, I don't think I've ever eaten a gooseberry,' he added dubiously.

'What?' She looked at him in surprise, before moving across the kitchen and returning with a white plastic bowl in her hand.

'Gooseberry fool is pure comfort food. You'll love it!' she told him firmly, handing him the bowl and giving him directions on where to find the bushes in the walled kitchen garden at the side of the house.

Gina was highly amused, and also considerably surprised, to discover that Antonio—whom she'd always thought of as a typically proud Spanish male—had allowed himself to be ordered around by a woman! But, to her astonishment, he'd gone off, as meek as a lamb, to pick the fruit for supper.

However, it did give her the opportunity to get on and do some cooking, without the pressure of his tall, dark presence looming over her in the kitchen.

'That was utterly delicious,' he said some considerable time later, putting down his spoon before reaching over to pour her another glass of dessert wine. 'Not only was it a beautifully composed meal, but clearly I must now add gooseberry purée whipped up in cream to the list of my favourite dishes.'

'I'm glad you enjoyed it,' she murmured, leaning back in her chair and smiling at him across the table in the dining room.

It was a lovely warm summer evening. The French windows were open out on to the terrace, their thin gauzy curtains billowing gently in a light evening breeze. The candles on the table were providing a softly intimate mood, the gentle flickering light contributing to an atmosphere of contentment and harmony.

Gina was astonished to discover just how much she'd enjoyed herself this evening. In fact, she'd been surprised to discover that, for the second time in twenty-four hours, Antonio had turned out to be the sort of guest about whom most hostesses could only dream: charming, attentive and highly entertaining.

Not only had he been highly appreciative of the food—always an important point, as far as the cook was concerned!—but he'd also kept her amused with stories and anecdotes, mostly about his past life as a successful lawyer in Madrid.

Unlike last night, when she'd been far too uptight and nervous, she had felt far more confident when sitting at her own dining room table, and had sought further news of his family. How amazing to think that Isabella, the older of his two sisters—who'd been a young girl, newly engaged to a rather dull fiancé when they'd last met—should now be the proud mother of three little daughters.

'No sons, as yet,' Antonio had told her with a slight shrug, before adding that, since his sister was expecting another baby, her husband, Jaime, was of course still hoping that they'd have a boy.

'Of course,' she'd echoed with a slight grin, recalling the importance many Continentals, especially the Italian and Spanish, placed on the birth of a son and heir.

However, leaning back in her chair now, and wondering whether she ought to go and make some coffee, Gina suddenly remembered a question she'd thought of asking Antonio earlier in the day, but which the discovery of his wine had sent completely out of her mind.

'I believe you saw my grandfather yesterday. He's

very elderly, and can't really face the journey to spend the weekend up here any more. And I've been terribly busy lately, and haven't been down to London as often as I'd wish. So...' She hesitated for a moment. 'I was wondering how you thought he was looking? To be honest,' she added with a rush, 'I've been rather worried about him. I didn't think he was looking at all well the last time we met.'

'Yes, as you know, I did see him yesterday,' Antonio said, also hesitating for a moment before adding, 'I was very sad to note that he was clearly not in the best of health.'

'You're quite right, he isn't. In fact, I'm very worried about him,' she confessed with a heavy sigh. 'But Grandpa just says that it's a case of old age—and that's something we're all going to suffer from sooner or later.'

Antonio gazed at the girl who was staring blindly down at her plate, clearly upset about the deteriorating health of a man who was, as far as he knew, her only living relative.

'Do you have any other members of your family— even distant cousins—who could maybe offer help and support if he became really ill?' Antonio asked quietly.

'Unfortunately, no, I don't.' Gina sighed. 'In fact, the only person remotely connected to me is my godmother, Joyce Frazer.'

'*Que?*'

'She's great! And a terrific character.' Gina grinned. 'I don't know exactly how she came to be my godmother, but she's always been there for me when I needed her. Joyce is a *very* wealthy widow, terrifically grand, and lives in a large house not very far away

from here. With masses of servants, wall to wall!' she
added with a laugh.

'But she and my grandfather don't really get on all
that well,' Gina continued, with a shrug of her slim
shoulders. 'I've often wondered if that could be because they're too alike... Although they're always
very polite to one another, of course.'

There was a slight pause as Antonio sipped his wine
and considered the problem.

Gina might be young and inexperienced as far as
business was concerned. But from one or two com-
ments she'd made during the evening he suspected that
beneath that pretty face and sparkling blue eyes there
lay a shrewd and perceptive mind. And, while he
wouldn't wish to dismiss the heaviness of the burden,
Antonio felt certain that she was quite strong enough
to cope with the unhappy days which lay ahead if
anything should happen to her grandfather.

Slowly revolving the slim stem of a crystal wine
glass between his long tanned fingers, Antonio said
quietly, 'Your grandfather does, of course, have a
point. We must all eventually grow old, *no*?'

'Yes.' Gina nodded.

'So...what is likely to happen to Brandon's of Pall
Mall when your grandfather is...er...no longer around
to run the business?' he queried gently.

'Goodness knows!' she told him with a slight shrug.

Buried in thought for a moment, she slowly realised
that the man sitting opposite her had also found himself facing the same problems as she did. That he'd
been forced to unexpectedly take over and run a family business. And was therefore well able to understand the many difficulties which she knew lay ahead
of her.

'The fact is that my grandfather still has the reins of the business very firmly in his own hands,' she said at last. 'And, although he's intending to leave me the business, I'm *really* in no hurry to take it on!

'However,' she added, 'I don't think he quite realises the problems of suddenly finding oneself in the driving seat, so to speak, without first having learnt to switch on the car's engine!'

'Ah!' Antonio smiled across the table at her, pleased to note that his judgement of this girl's general acumen and good sense had been correct. 'I take it that you mean you really should have some experience in learning to run the business before being ultimately responsible for the firm?'

'Precisely!' She nodded. 'Even if I wished to interfere—which I most certainly do not—my grandfather simply isn't capable of delegating the day-to-day running of the business. Although, to be fair, he did make sure that I had some considerable experience of working under him, at the office in Pall Mall, before coming up to take charge of the local branch here in Ipswich.'

She paused for a moment. 'I suppose it's only natural that he shouldn't want to let go. After all, he's been running the business since the year dot. So he's bound to think that no one else can do it as well as he can. And, to be quite honest, he's probably quite right!' she added with a rueful smile.

'Well...it seems to me that there is nothing you can do about the problem at the moment,' Antonio told her. 'As for the future...? Who knows what might happen? It is, after all, quite possible that you might marry a man who'd be able to help and support you in the business.'

She gave a slight shrug of her shoulders. 'Anything is possible,' she told him. 'But I'm in no hurry to settle down. I mean…I've still got an awful lot to learn about the wine business. Besides,' she added with a grin, 'at twenty-six I'm hardly on the shelf! And what about you?'

'Me?' He blinked, a brief, startled expression flickering across his tanned face for a moment.

'Yes—you!' She grinned. 'There's no need to look so surprised. You must be…what?…about thirty-four by now? Which, I must admit, does sound as if you've got at least one foot in the grave!'

'Thank you, Gina!' he laughed.

'Well—are you married?'

'No. No, I am not,' he told her firmly.

'What? Not even a fiancée…or two?' she teased, feeling slightly giddy and light-headed.

'Ah, well…' He grinned. 'Maybe there was a "fiancée or two", as you put it, in the past. But the sad truth is that I lost my heart to someone a very long time ago,' he added slowly, staring down into his glass of wine. 'Unfortunately, the circumstances were… well, let us just say that they were difficult.'

'Oh, dear. Was she married?'

He gave a slight shrug of his broad shoulders. 'These things happen. However, that is all well in the past, when I was young and very foolish. Fortunately, time takes care of most problems. And maybe, as I said earlier, you may find a husband who will be a help and support to you when you finally take over your grandfather's business.'

'Well…' She wrinkled her nose. 'It depends how you define "helpful", doesn't it? I certainly don't want to get hitched to some boring old accountant!'

'No indeed!' he drawled, leaning back in his chair and allowing his glinting dark eyes to flicker over the delicious curves of the girl sitting opposite him. 'Especially, my dear Gina, when it is clearly obvious to me that a very beautiful girl such as yourself would have no problem in finding a husband.'

Giving him a brief smile, and wishing that she was better at accepting compliments, Gina was painfully aware of the deep flush rising up over cheeks.

'And in any case—' Antonio shrugged '—you might already be deeply in love with someone whom you would hope to marry in the future. Hmm?'

'No, there's no one special in my life at the moment,' she told him firmly.

'But I imagine that you must have had many boyfriends, *no*?'

'Well...yes, of course I have,' she retorted quickly, definitely not prepared to let this devastating, highly attractive man think that no one had ever fancied her!

'And at least two of them wanted to marry me!' she added defiantly.

And then, as he gave a low, sexy laugh, she could feel her cheeks burning again as she realised that she must sound a complete idiot.

Oh, Lord! Maybe she'd drunk too much wine? Because, during the last few hours, when they'd been sitting talking and laughing companionably together, she'd felt totally relaxed and at ease.

But now...now the atmosphere between them suddenly seemed to be crackling with hidden tension. Just as it had earlier in the day, in that dark old cellar beneath the shop. A highly-charged aura of sexual tension, which had the effect of making her feel extraordinarily nervous and ill at ease.

She was finding it almost impossible to tear her gaze away from the disturbing gleam in his dark eyes; their glittering depths carried a message which she didn't quite understand, but which seemed to be prompting a deep tide of excitement to begin flowing through her veins.

As she stared at Antonio, leaning casually back in his chair and smiling across the table at her as he slowly sipped his glass of wine, there seemed no obvious or logical reason why her heart should suddenly start pounding like a sledgehammer out of control. Or why prickles of apprehension should be tingling up and down the length of her spine...

Oh, dear! She *really* shouldn't have drunk so much wine—it definitely seemed to have made her acutely aware of Antonio's strong, raw sexuality. So it had clearly been asking for trouble not to watch her intake of alcohol as carefully as he'd been doing. Although, of course, it was different in Antonio's case, since he was going to be driving back to London later tonight.

But...but all she could think about was the woman to whom he'd apparently lost his heart many years ago. Did he still care for her? And...and why should she be feeling so sick about it if he did?

Coffee! That was what she needed. Lots and *lots* of strong coffee, Gina told herself, as Antonio excused himself for a moment, and she quickly made her way to the kitchen.

As much caffeine as she could manage to absorb— if the fumes of alcohol now swirling around in her brain were anything to go by.

So...OK, she'd been an idiot to drink so much tonight, but that had surely been understandable? It wasn't every day that your long-lost love suddenly appeared out of the blue. And he'd turned out to be every bit as attractive as he had been all that time ago. And Antonio had already caused her enough grief and unhappiness to last a lifetime. She definitely couldn't face another long period while she tried to get over the disastrous effect he appeared to have on her frail emotions.

In fact, you stupid fool, you've allowed him to charm the socks off you, she castigated herself bitterly, as she carried the tray of coffee into the large sitting room.

But knowing that she'd been a total idiot, caving in this evening to his dark enchantment, and falling a willing victim to the beguiling, almost irresistible force of his overwhelming attraction, was one thing. How she was going to deal with it once he'd driven back to London was quite another.

The main thing, she decided, pouring herself a large cup of black coffee, was to try and keep her end up. To make sure that she gave him no hint or reason to suppose that she was anything but an extremely sophisticated woman of the world. One who'd been pleased to see an old flame, and had, in fact, thoroughly enjoyed his company, both last night and today. But who was also perfectly calm and totally relaxed about the fact that she might never see him again.

Yes—that was *definitely* the way to handle the situation. Unfortunately it was easier said than done, she realised, just as Antonio came into the room.

'Ah, I thought I caught the delicious scent of fresh coffee,' he said, coming over to sit down on the sofa beside her. 'I've just been out to the car to use my mobile phone.'

'Oh, yes?' she murmured as she concentrated on pouring him some coffee. 'Did you have any problem getting through?'

'No, none at all,' he told her coolly, his dark eyes glinting with sardonic amusement as he took the cup and saucer from her hands. Which, he noted with interest, were shaking slightly, clearly betraying the fact that Miss Gina Brandon was not *quite* as cool and composed as she seemed.

And that was merely a case of rough justice, he told himself firmly. Because, thanks to the effect of that quite outrageously sexy dress, he'd had considerable problems himself this evening. Principally in keeping his own hands off this lovely girl's ravishing figure!

A silence fell on the room as Gina stared down at the black liquid in her cup, trying to avoid looking at the man now sitting so close to her. She seemed to be having trouble breathing and she could almost feel her pulse positively racing out of control.

'Would you like some more coffee?' she muttered huskily, doing her level best to ignore the long, muscular thigh touching her own as he leaned forward to place his cup down on the low table in front of them.

'No, I think I've had enough. Especially as I'm not driving back to London tonight.'

'You're not...not going back to London?' Startled, Gina turned to face him.

Antonio gave a shrug of his broad shoulders. 'I decided it was probably best not to. Which is why I've just phoned up my hotel there and cancelled my reservation for tonight. It seemed sensible, since I suspect that I may have drunk more than was wise tonight.'

'But...but I noticed that you hardly touched any wine. Which is why I thought...well, it seems I was obviously wrong...' she muttered helplessly, before taking another quick sip of coffee and trying to pummel her sluggish mind into some kind of working order.

'So, you...er...you'd like to stay on here, in the house...?'

He grinned. 'As an alternative to sleeping in my car? Yes, indeed I would!'

'Well...OK.' She sighed as he leaned back on the cushions and smiled at her.

She really didn't know whether to be sorry or glad that he'd decided not to return to London. It would mean that he'd still be around for part of tomorrow, at least. But she was rapidly beginning to think that wasn't a good idea. Not when merely one of those beguilingly seductive smiles could have such a mesmerising effect on her emotions.

'It has been a delightful evening,' he said, his deep voice cutting into her disordered thoughts. 'But now I think that it is about time we went to bed. Don't you?'

'Yes, I suppose so,' she murmured, trying to pull herself together. 'You know where your room is, of course.'

'*My* room...?' he drawled with sardonic amusement. 'Oh, no, *querida*. I am not at all interested in that. *Absolutamente, no!*'

'What...?' She turned to stare at his tanned, handsome face, her mind in a total whirl. 'Are you suggesting...?'

'That I wish to go to bed with you? But, yes—of course I do! Is it so surprising that I should want to make love to such a warm, beautiful woman?' he murmured, casually sliding his arm along the back of the sofa.

'But…but…you can't just swan in here…thinking that you can pick up where you left off eight years ago!' she cried. 'And…and… Hey! Cut that out!' she snapped, as he raised his hand and she felt him plucking the combs from her hair.

'Whatever happened in the past, I have never…*ever* forgotten your glorious, wonderful long hair,' he murmured as the heavy mass tumbled down over her shoulders.

'Oh—for heaven's sake!' she muttered, her hands fluttering helplessly while trying to both scoop up her hair and push him away, as he lowered his arm to encircle her waist, drawing her slowly towards him.

'P-please, Antonio—you don't understand!' she gasped, shivering as he raised his other hand, winding his fingers through the tresses of her pale gold hair. 'I'm *not* the silly…stupid girl you knew all those years ago.'

'Indeed you are not!' he agreed with a low rumble of husky laughter, his hand tightening in her hair and holding her head firmly beneath him, tilting it back against the cushions so that she found herself gazing up into his handsome, tanned face.

Goodness knows what was happening to her…that was one of the few coherent thoughts flooding through her brain, and her sapphire-blue eyes widened in her pale face as she gazed helplessly up at the hard, sensual line of his mouth. Her head seemed to be pounding with a strange fever, and although she knew… hoped…feared…that he was going to kiss her, she couldn't seem to move. It was as though she was trapped in a weird, hypnotic trance, totally mesmerised by the intense, fiery glitter in his sparkling dark eyes.

And then, as if in slow motion, he gradually lowered

his dark head, his mouth taking possession of hers and parting her quivering, trembling lips to allow his tongue to invade the soft, inner sweetness of her mouth with ruthless determination. She was barely aware of moaning helplessly as he lowered her back against the plump sofa cushions. His hands were sweeping over her body, his strong fingers erotically caressing her soft curves with a mounting, hungry passion which left her utterly dazed and trembling in his arms.

As his lips softened, moving over her mouth with a slow, languorous sensuality, they provoked a wanton, passionate response in her trembling body which she seemed powerless to deny. And how could she? When this was all she'd ever wanted...all she'd ever dreamed of...since first setting eyes on him all those years ago.

And yet...the past now seemed a different country, and of no relevance to the present. Now...now she was a fully mature woman, with every fibre of her being consumed by a rushing tide of fierce pleasure and excitement, relishing the strong arousal of the hard, firm body pressed so closely to her own, the rapid pounding of his heart and the scorching heat of his mouth. And almost of their own volition her arms closed about his neck, her fingers feverishly burying themselves in his thick, black hair as she fervently responded to the electrifying intoxication of his kiss.

Aeons of time seemed to pass before he slowly raised his head, gazing intently down at the sweet, quivering temptation of her lips, at the dazed blue eyes staring helplessly up at him, totally in thrall to the storm of passion and desire rampaging through her body.

'*Querida...!*' he groaned softly, his lips twisted in a briefly mocking smile, before burying his face in her long hair for a moment. 'I think we *are* most surely going to bed...together. *No?*'

'Oh, Lord—I sincerely hope so!' she gasped, not fully realising that she'd spoken her instantaneous thoughts out loud until she heard him give a deep growl of laughter.

And then, with what seemed effortless ease, he smoothly rose from the sofa, raising her limp, trembling body in his arms, before swiftly leaving the room and mounting the wide, curving staircase to her bedroom.

CHAPTER FOUR

'I...I'M NOT sure that this is such a good idea after all...' Gina muttered nervously as he lowered her gently down on to the bed, suddenly swamped by feelings of deep apprehension.

She liked to think that she was a reasonably sophisticated woman, who'd had her share of boyfriends and lovers. But...she'd had so many fantasies over the years about making love with Antonio that the reality was bound to be a great disappointment. And she wasn't sure that she could bear that.

'A good idea?' Antonio gazed down at her in astonishment for a moment, before giving a deep, husky laugh as he sat down on the bed beside her.

'Ah, *querida*—cannot you see? Surely you *must* know that, good idea or not, I have been thinking of little else other than wanting to make love to you since I arrived here yesterday.'

'Really?'

'*Sí—ciertamente!*' he said firmly, the sensual mockery in his brief smile and the glittering darkness of his eyes causing her heart to give a dangerous lurch as he put out a hand to gently brush a coil of hair from her brow.

'We have a history that goes back a long way, *no*? But that was when we were both much younger,' he added softly, as his warm fingers moved over her cheek and down down her long neck. 'You were just out of school. While I...? I was nothing but a callow youth who should have known better than to play with fire.'

She suddenly found herself feeling deeply touched, both by Antonio's honesty and the genuine sincerity and regret in his voice as he acknowledged his part in that unhappy episode. And she, who had been so pre-occupied all these years with her *own* hurt, could now almost physically feel the cold icy fingers which had encased her frozen heart for so long slowly melting beneath the warmth of his smile.

'It wasn't all your fault,' she admitted with a slight sigh. 'I was…well, I was a very silly young girl. Stuffed full of romantic nonsense from reading too many Victorian novels.'

'Ah, *no*! You were charming. So sweet. So inno-cent,' he murmured, ignoring her slight gasp as his hand slowly trailed down over the fine bones and soft skin of her bare shoulders, lightly brushing aside the thin straps of her dress to expose her breasts. 'As for what happened? Well, I very soon came to bitterly regret my stupid behaviour.'

But Gina was finding it increasingly difficult to con-centrate on what he was saying. The warmth of his long, tanned fingers moving enticingly over the hard-ening tips of her bare breasts was almost driving her to distraction. And when he lowered his dark head, his mouth closing possessively over one enlarged, swollen nipple, she gave a helpless moan as a stream of elec-trifying, fiery excitement zigzagged through her body.

'So…we will make love, *no*…?' he breathed huskily against her skin, before his warm lips trailed a scorching path over her quivering flesh towards her other breast.

'*Oh, yes!*' she gasped, impatiently helping him as

he removed her dress and panties, before he swiftly
unbuttoned his shirt. Tossing it and the rest of his
clothes aside, he slipped into bed beside her, his warm
arms tenderly enfolding her trembling body.

'Mmm...you smell wonderful!' he murmured, his
voice husky with desire, before kissing her very
gently, as if she was something rare and precious, his
lips seeming to carry a magic spell as they trailed
slowly down over her face and neck to her breasts.
The touch of his mouth brushing against her nipples
sent shivers of excitement dancing across her skin
once more; the feel of his warm lips and hands moving
down over her body, carefully savouring every inch of
her quivering, naked flesh, almost drove her wild with
desire.

For the first time in her life she could feel her emotions spinning totally out of control. And she simply
couldn't care less!

By now firmly in the grip of a languorous, wanton
force as old as time itself, she surrendered to the need
to run her trembling hands through the dark curly hair
of his broad chest, sliding her fingers over the contours
of his firm, muscular body and on down the smooth
line of his back, revelling in the sound of his sharp
intake of breath as her touch became more enticing,
more intimate.

'Dios...!' he muttered hoarsely against her skin.
The deep, huskily sensual note in his voice inflaming
her desire. 'How did I not know it would be like this?'

As his hands moved slowly over her flesh, exploring
every soft curve and crevice, she felt as if she was
drowning in ecstasy; his lips and tongue stroked her,
leading her upwards towards some far-off land of bliss
and passion. The helpless moans of a voice which she

barely recognised as her own were echoing in her ears as the excitement increased to become a frenzy deep inside her. And then she was suddenly gripped by a seemingly endless series of ever-mounting convulsions, soaring up into the stratosphere on wings of sheer rapture and delight such as she had never dreamed existed.

It was only then that his strong, muscular figure swiftly covered hers with a fierce urgency. The dynamically hard, forceful thrusts of his powerful body were vigorously propelling them both towards a shattering climax, until he, too, groaned out loud in the release and ecstasy of their mutual fulfilment.

Much later, as she lay wrapped in his arms, Gina was still feeling totally dazed by Antonio's lovemaking, which far and away transcended anything she'd ever experienced. Or anything she could have imagined, she told herself with a deep sigh of utter contentment, before she slowly drifted off into a dreamless sleep.

When she finally awoke, still firmly cradled in his arms, it was to see the bright morning sun pouring in through the windows—she and Antonio clearly having been far too absorbed with one another last night to even think of drawing the curtains.

Lying still for a while, quietly aware of the strong, rhythmic beat of his heart, she hadn't realised he was also awake until he whispered in her ear. 'You made me a very happy man last night, my darling Gina. And you? You were happy, too?'

'Oh, well...' She grinned up at the ceiling. 'I suppose I *could* say that I wasn't *too* unhappy... But I'd be lying!' she added quickly, as he raised his dark head to glare down at her. 'Oh, come on, Antonio,' she laughed. 'Surely you don't need me to tell you that you're a sensational lover?'

'Of course I do!' he retorted with a broad smile. 'I am a man, *no*? But...since you appear to have doubts about my sexual prowess...' He gave a heavily dramatic sigh. 'Well, it seems that I have no choice but to try and convince you that I am at least, as you say in this country, "better than sliced bread"!'

'No...really...Antonio! For heaven's sake—I was only joking!' she gasped, as she felt his hands beginning to move slowly and sensually over her body.

'Too late!' he murmured huskily, his strong arms tightening possessively about her slim body as he drew her up against him. 'Ah, *querida*! How wonderfully soft your skin is...as smooth as silk,' he breathed, obviously savouring every moment as his hands moved slowly and leisurely over her warm, pliant flesh towards the round peaks of her breasts, swollen and aching for his touch.

Becoming aware of the rising heat of his body, pressed so closely to her own, she was swept by a fierce and overwhelming compulsion to respond to his increasingly urgent touch; every inch of her flesh was quivering and vibrating in response to his sensual arousal. And then suddenly, from almost out of nowhere, savagely raw passion seemed to explode passionately between them, their bodies merging in a wild, untamed hunger and overpowering need for one another.

'*Strewth!*' Gina muttered some time later as she became aware of Antonio levering himself back up against the pillows beside her. 'I'm not sure I can take much more of this lovemaking Spanish-style! But I'm happy to give you a signed testimonial to the effect that you're *definitely* better than sliced bread!'

Antonio laughed, before swinging his long legs off the bed and striding over to the window, throwing it open and taking deep breaths as he stretched his long, tall frame.

'Thank goodness the Lamberts are away for the weekend,' Gina giggled, gazing at his naked, superbly fit, tanned figure. 'Poor Doris, our housekeeper, would probably have a heart attack if she could see you now!' she added, languorously stretching her own satiated body and preparing to drift off to sleep once more.

But Antonio clearly had other ideas.

'Come on, sleepy-head!' he said, coming over to pull the sheets down from her protesting figure. 'It is time to get up. We must go shopping.'

'*Shopping?*' she groaned, reluctantly sitting up in bed and raising her arms to brush her hands through the long, tangled coils of her pale hair.

'Ah, *querida*!' he murmured, lowering himself down on to the bed beside her and running his hand over her warm, soft body, savouring her slim waist and those wonderfully firm full breasts. 'I am almost tempted…but, no—shopping it must be!'

'But I don't understand.' She frowned up at him in puzzlement. 'What's with this sudden desire to hit the shops?'

'Really, Gina!' he exclaimed, rising to his feet, clearly surprised at her question. 'I must buy some clothes, of course.'

'Clothes?'

'You will recall that I was only intending to stay here, with you, for one night? Which means that I have left most of my luggage in the hotel in London. And I cannot possibly be expected to wear, for the whole of today, the shirt and trousers which I wore yesterday,' he told her firmly.

'Oh, well—I suppose you're right,' she acknowledged.

'So, while I go and have a shower in the guest suite, I expect you to immediately rise and get ready to leave the house as soon as possible,' he said, swiftly gathering up the clothes he'd discarded last night before leaving the room.

'By the way,' he added, popping his head back round the door to give her an engaging smile. 'When you are making breakfast, I would like some of your English toasts, with lots of marmalade, and a large pot of black coffee.'

As his dark head disappeared from sight once more Gina reluctantly scrambled off the bed, muttering under her breath about male chauvinist pigs as she made her way into her adjoining bathroom.

What did he think this was—a first class hotel? Still...there was no getting away from the fact that the damn man was, without any shadow of doubt, the most *fantastic* lover! Never, in all her life, had she been raised to such ecstatic heights of rapturous happiness.

And, quite honestly, she told herself with a grin as she turned on the shower, what did fixing him a simple breakfast matter when compared to their wonderful night of utter bliss? And the fact that he was clearly intending to stay here, with her, for at least the rest of today was enough to set her heart positively fizzing with joy.

Caught up in the whirlwind of what appeared to be

Antonio's idea of how to conduct a shopping expedition, Gina found herself feeling totally dazed by the time they returned to the car.

Driving around the town of Ipswich, situated on the banks of the River Orwell, he'd been particularly interested in viewing the ancient buildings of the old East Anglian town.

'I was too busy, yesterday, to appreciate the local architecture,' he'd explained, insisting on stopping the car, in the middle of the busy Saturday traffic, to admire the highly ornate plasterwork on some of the old houses.

'Well, it may be interesting. But I think we're going to be arrested any minute if we don't get out of here,' she'd told him, flinching at the noise of angry horns and bellows of rage from the other vehicles jammed in the narrow street behind them.

Hurriedly directing him to the car park in the centre of the town, near the Butter Market, she'd found herself being dragged around the various shops and boutiques at what seemed the speed of light. However, it had given her an opportunity to pop into a supermarket and stock up with some basic groceries.

Antonio's idea of 'shopping', together with his imperious manner—and, she suspected, his outstanding good looks—seemed to bring assistants running at the double in practically every shop they entered. And while he might not be the easiest customer to deal with he sure as heck was a fast one!

'Are you certain that you've done *enough* shopping for one day?' she queried sarcastically now, as they loaded what seemed like a mountain of bags on to the back seat of the car.

'Possibly not—but that will have to do,' he said,

merely grinning at the heavy irony in her voice as he
settled into the driver's seat, impatiently drumming his
fingers on the wheel as he waited for her to do up her
seat belt. 'Do you spend much of your life shopping?'

'Good heavens, no!' she muttered, wrestling with
the thick webbing, whose buckle was obstinately refusing to fit into its slot. 'I'm one of those freaks of
nature who absolutely *loathes* having to trail around
shops. As far as I'm concerned it's total purgatory—
and an amazing waste of time.'

He laughed, switching on the engine, as she at last
succeeded in fixing her seat belt, and drawing the vehicle out into the heavy Saturday morning traffic.

'If that is so, you must be the *only* woman of my
acquaintance, my dear Gina, who does not spend at
least half her life in a shopping arcade!'

However, once they'd arrived back at Bradgate
Manor, it seemed that Antonio had programmed the
rest of the day as firmly as he'd arranged their trip to
Ipswich. And Gina, who was used to making her own
decisions, was amazed to find herself meekly agreeing
to his plans.

Having noted, on the day of his arrival, the presence
of an elderly mare in the stable next to Pegasus, he
had nodded understandingly when she'd explained that
she kept the old horse specifically as a companion for
the other animal.

And so, on their return from town, he imperiously
decided that they would saddle up the two horses and
take them out for a short ride through the bridle paths
of the surrounding countryside. But of course, as she
might have guessed, Antonio had no intention of allowing her to ride Pegasus.

'This old mare is far more suitable for you,' he said

firmly, merely grinning at the scowl on her face as he gave her a quick lift up into the saddle.

'I don't see why I can't ride my own horse, for heaven's sake!' she grumbled as he sprang lightly up on to the back of the larger animal.

'Because, my darling, I cannot face the prospect of nearly having a heart attack, like I did on my arrival! And if this large brute thinks that he's going to be able to bolt back to his stable with *me* on his back—he's going to find that he's very much mistaken! And you must admit,' he added with a laugh, 'I am far too tall to ride the mare. With my feet practically on the ground, I would look a fool, *no*?'

'Fair enough,' she agreed. Although, gazing at the tall figure sitting so confidently astride the large horse, wearing a casual short-sleeved light blue shirt and a pair of tight blue jeans which he'd purchased earlier this morning, Gina found herself thinking that he looked totally magnificent—and even more sexually attractive than ever as he cantered off down the lane in front of her.

As they rode happily together through the fields and woods surrounding the village, Gina honestly couldn't remember when she'd ever felt quite so happy. It seemed difficult to comprehend that it was only two days ago that Antonio had suddenly turned up out of the blue. However strange it might seem, it really did feel as if he'd been there for ever.

Primarily, of course, they seemed to have so much to talk about. And, then again, they had so much in common. Since they'd both lost their parents when young, and had been raised by elderly grandparents, he clearly understood her recollection of times in the past when she'd been incredibly lonely, despite the loving care and attention of her grandparents.

'I was luckier than you, my dear Gina, since I had two younger sisters as companions,' he mused quietly as they dismounted from their horses to enable her to show him around the ancient village church. 'But, since I was the eldest child by some years, I can well understand the problems you faced.'

And, of course, as he talked about taking over the running of the business following his uncle's death, she realised that they also shared a very strong bond—of having been raised by families intimately involved in the wine trade.

'I know what you mean,' she murmured reflectively. 'Although our backgrounds are very different, of course, there are some important aspects which we have in common.'

'Indeed there are!' His eyes gleamed with amusement. 'The fact that we both find shopping a boring occupation is undoubtedly one of them. And let us not forget one or two others—such as our extraordinary compatibility in bed, for instance, not to mention...'

'Oh—for heaven's sake!' she muttered, her lips curving into a slightly embarrassed grin. She wasn't used to discussing such matters so openly and freely, and couldn't seem to prevent a deep flush rising up over her pale cheeks.

'Ah, *querida*! I love teasing you. You rise to the bait every time!' He grinned as they remounted their horses. 'Where to now?'

'I thought we'd go down this part of the main road, and then through a gate over there,' she said, raising a hand to point it out to him. 'It's the entrance to an old bridle path leading back to the Manor, and will give us a chance for a good gallop before reaching home.'

'*Bueno.*' He nodded, leading the way down the road in front of her.

Just as he was leaning down to open the gate Gina became aware of the sound of a large limousine approaching them. However, after making sure that she drew her horse on to the verge, she was ignoring the approaching vehicle when she heard someone calling out her name. Turning around in the saddle, she immediately recognised the huge and very grand, if decidedly ancient, Rolls Royce.

'Hello, darling! It's a lovely day for a ride, isn't it?' her godmother, Joyce Frazer, called out through the open window at the rear of the vehicle, before imperiously instructing her chauffeur to halt the car.

'Yes, it's a glorious day,' Gina agreed, walking her horse up to the vehicle as the chauffeur came around to open the door, allowing her godmother to step out into the road.

'Well…you're certainly looking very well, darling,' Joyce told her, before turning her eyes towards Antonio, who, having opened the gate, was clearly waiting for Gina to join him.

'Good heavens!' the older woman exclaimed, her eyes widening as she viewed the tall figure sitting astride his horse some yards away. 'What an *extraordinarily* handsome man,' she added with a slight laugh. 'Where on earth did you find *him*?'

'He…er…he's been staying at the Manor for a few days. He is over here from Spain. On business,' Gina mumbled, bitterly aware of a flush spreading up over her cheeks beneath the amused, shrewd gaze of her godmother.

'Well...I clearly mustn't interrupt any "business" discussions,' Joyce murmured, her eyes twinkling with laughter. 'But I shall expect you to come and see me next week, and tell me *all* about this new friend of yours,' she said, getting back in the car and ordering her chauffeur to drive on.

Just my luck! Gina told herself gloomily as she rode back to join Antonio.

She knew that when she next saw Joyce, her god-mother would have the whole story out of her—in five seconds flat! And Gina hadn't cared for the way the chauffeur had been following their exchange with some considerable interest.

He'll be down the pub, telling his mates—and then the whole village will know all about it! That was the trouble with country life. Everyone knew everyone else's business!

However, after telling Antonio that she'd just been talking to her godmother—and making a mental note to keep well out of Joyce's way for as long as possi-ble—she did her best to put the whole incident out of her mind. It was a lovely day, and she was having far too much fun to worry about providing fodder for local gossip.

Indeed, by the time they returned to the house Gina thought that very far from being a stranger with whom she'd only been briefly acquainted in the past, Antonio now seemed an old and best friend whom she'd known all her life.

Which was why she hadn't the slightest hesitation in rapping him quickly over the knuckles with her wooden spoon when she caught him dipping a finger into the cucumber and dill sauce!

'Cut that out!' she told him with mock severity, moving the bowl out of his reach.

Clearly if she didn't keep a beady eye on him there'd be no sauce to go with the cold trout, which she'd cooked earlier, while he'd been having breakfast.

'Kindly remember,' she added sternly, 'There's no sampling of the food in *my* kitchen!'

'Umm...it tastes delicious,' he grinned at her. 'What are we having after the trout?'

'Oh, Lord—I don't know.' She shrugged. 'Will cheese do?'

'Cheese, yes. But what else?'

Putting her hands on her hips, Gina surveyed him with mock severity. 'Don't you ever think of *anything* other than food?'

'But, yes—of course I do!' He gave a low rumble of sensual laughter. 'I think of making love to you. And then maybe some food. And then I think of making love to you again!'

'Honestly! You're hopeless,' she muttered with a grin, turning back to continue whipping up the sauce.

But it was proving to be extremely difficult to concentrate on the job in hand. Her whole mind...her whole being...seemed caught up in the strong attraction he had for her, her mind filled with memories of the wild, totally mind-blowing way they'd made love, both last night and this morning. But...was it merely sex? Or did her feeling about him lie much deeper than that?

With her errant mind filled with images of their naked bodies lying entwined together, she wasn't able to prevent a flush rising up over her cheeks as he slipped his arms around her waist. As he pulled her back against his tall figure, she was left in doubt of his arousal as his hands swept up to firmly cup her full breasts.

'You see?' he breathed, lowering his dark head to press his lips to her neck. 'I cannot resist you, my darling—or your delicious food,' he added, holding her strongly clasped to him with one hand while reaching forward to dip his finger in the sauce once again.

'OK—that's it!' She laughed, breaking away from his embrace to hand him a white china bowl. 'Out of my kitchen—and don't come back until that bowl is full of strawberries from the kitchen garden.'

'Ah—no querida...'

'Go on! Shoo!' she told him firmly, laughingly pushing his reluctant figure towards the kitchen door. 'I've got some more cooking to do, and I still haven't had time to go upstairs and change out of these jodhpurs. So—off with you! Right now!'

'You're a hard woman, Gina,' he groaned dramatically as he opened the door.

'Absolutamente!' she agreed with a wide grin. 'And if a certain man of my acquaintance doesn't do as he's told, any idea of lunch—or making love, for that matter—will be strictly off the menu!'

Antonio might be an impatient man, and, she suspected, potentially difficult and tricky to live with, but you had to hand it to him, Gina told herself as the light lunch she'd prepared came to its end, he was certainly a pleasure to cook for.

Clearly interested in the combination of different herbs in the sauce, he'd taken an appreciative and lively interest in the various dishes which had been placed in front of him. Even that good old English standby, fresh strawberries and cream.

And he was looking very tasty, too, she thought, her eyes drifting over his short-sleeved shirt, open at the neck to display the curly black hairs at the base of his throat...before almost laughing out loud at *just* how much she seemed to have changed over the past few days.

Before his sudden reappearance in her life she'd never have *dreamed* of referring to any man in such a way. And yet...well, there was no getting away from the fact that when he was anywhere near her she could feel herself positively fizzing with excitement.

Despite trying to keep a clear mind, she couldn't seem to think of anything other than the delights and pleasures of his hard, muscular body. In fact, she appeared to be totally enslaved by the rampant, highly potent aura of raw sex appeal which seemed to ooze from every pore of his impressively handsome figure.

And then, recalling the question she'd asked herself earlier, in the kitchen, she realised with a shock that it seemed she really *had* fallen in love with Antonio.

Not the fairy-tale version of love, which had so consumed her much younger, adolescent self. No, the fact was that they were currently 'in lust', and practically unable to keep their hands off each other. And, most surprisingly of all, this was definitely *not* the way she'd ever expected to feel when truly in love with another human being.

It seemed to consist of a total certainty that Antonio was the one man for her. And that this fully mature, deep, emotional response had always been waiting for her, just out of sight, for a very long time. Ever since she'd first set eyes on him, all those years ago.

'Gina...?'

'Oh, sorry—I was daydreaming,' she muttered, be-

fore quickly making a determined effort to try and pull
herself together.

Rising from her chair, she began stacking their
plates on the sideboard before their removal to the
kitchen. 'Would you like some coffee?'

'No,' he murmured, after a quick glance down at
the thin gold watch on his wrist. 'No—I think it is
now time for us to have a *siesta*!'

'A *siesta*?' She gazed at him in surprise. 'But we
don't have a rest after lunch here in England.'

'That is clearly a great mistake,' he announced with
a wolfish grin as he rose from the table, adamantly
refusing to let her wash up the dishes. 'Unlike myself—they can wait!' he added firmly, walking slowly
towards her.

Once again, the sharp, insistent tug of sexual aware-
ness seemed to be causing havoc with her nervous
system. It was as if she was paralysed. Incapable of
movement. Trapped by the gleam of those glittering
dark eyes and unable to tear her gaze away from the
sensual curve of his mouth as he came to a halt beside
her.

'I prefer your hair to flow free...' he murmured,
sliding a warm hand around the back of her neck while
he removed the combs pinning the heavy knot to the
crown of her head.

Shivering helplessly as he slowly ran his long,
tanned fingers through the rippling stream of her pale
blonde hair, she could feel his hands sliding down her
back, pressing her firmly up against him as he lowered
his dark head, brushing his lips gently over her brow,
before trailing them slowly down to the corner of her
quivering mouth. So slowly that she was breathless

and trembling, as if in the grip of a fever, before he eventually possessed her lips with a force and passion which swiftly drove her almost frantic with desire.

Was this really her true self? Gina wondered bemusedly as she felt his hands swiftly sliding her light cotton skirt up over her thighs. Had she really become this wanton creature, exulting in her power to arouse him as he gripped her tightly and lifted her up against him? Utterly shameless as she coiled her arms about his neck, winding her legs about his hips and revelling in the exciting movements of his tall body as he carried her upstairs to the bedroom.

'And don't tell me this is *not* a good idea...' he growled, setting her lightly down on her feet.

'I wouldn't dream of it!' she gasped.

'*Bueno!*' He gave a deep, husky grunt of laughter, before impatiently pulling her towards him and once more possessing her lips in a kiss of devastating intensity.

It seemed as if they were both firmly in the grip of the same madness, feverishly stripping the clothes from one another before sinking down on to the bed in a wild tangle of arms and legs, totally overcome by a primitive force that was clearly beyond their control.

And then...then there was no more time to think, as she found herself going up in flames, moaning feverishly as their raw and untamed, overpowering hunger and need for one another drove her almost to the edge of sanity, before he buried himself deep inside her, the hard, pulsating rhythm gradually building to a violent explosion as they merged to become one entity in a wild, ecstatic torrent of passion and desire.

*   *   *

Much later, lying warm and drowsily replete, Gina put out a hand to touch Antonio—only to find that he was no longer in the bed beside her.

Idly wondering where he'd got to, she threw back the sheets and slipped out of bed, moving slowly around the room, picking up the clothes which she had so wildly abandoned an hour or two ago.

Pausing to stare out of one of the windows, she saw that Antonio was walking slowly up and down the wide lawn just outside the house.

Gazing down at him she could feel her heart give a sudden lurch. Oh, Lord! What *was* she going to do when he left here? As he was bound to do, very soon. Because he had a business, and a life to lead in Spain—just as she had her own responsibilities, both to her grandfather and her career in the wine trade, here in England. So, any half-baked idea she might have that these few days were anything more than a brief, happy interlude in their busy lives was downright stupid.

Unfortunately for her, Gina knew that she was already fathoms deep in love with Antonio. And, although it was going to break her heart, she also knew that their relationship was doomed to wither and die—sooner rather than later.

Oh, yes…they might manage to spend a weekend or two together, if and when he could spare the time from his business responsibilities. But that was obviously the most she could hope for. And, even then, such a long-distance relationship wasn't likely to survive the logistical difficulties of living in two quite separate countries.

Feeling immeasurably sad and bereft at having forced herself to face the harsh, stark reality of her situation, Gina realised that she must quickly pull herself together. Although Antonio clearly couldn't remain here for very long, it would be foolish not to concentrate on enjoying what little time they had left together.

Deciding to take her own advice, concentrating on the present while letting the future take care of itself, really had been a good idea, Gina told herself later in the evening as she and Antonio sat talking, nineteen to the dozen, after enjoying another happy meal together.

And later, upstairs in her bedroom, there was no room for feelings of sadness and regret. Only increasing delight and overwhelming happiness as he made long, slow, delicious love to her, with such tender warmth and intensity that it far transcended anything she'd ever known before. As she sank beneath the tidal waves of overwhelming passion and desire it seemed to her that they had become one flesh and one soul, with the universe seeming to explode about them in brilliant, searing fragments of fiery light and power.

Not being at her best first thing in the morning, it took Gina some time to realise that Antonio—clearly someone who liked to be up with the lark—was, nevertheless, acting very much out of character.

'Good heavens!' she mumbled sleepily as she sat up against the pillows, brushing the tangled hair from her face as she stared in astonishment at the man standing beside the bed.

Gazing bemusedly at the large tray containing a hot pot of coffee, a boiled egg and several pieces of toast, she could only shake her head in wonder.

'I didn't know that you were capable of even boiling a kettle,' she exclaimed. 'Let alone providing me with breakfast in bed!'

'I'll have you know that I am a man of many talents,' he told her loftily, placing the tray on a small table beside the bed and pouring them both a large cup of coffee.

'Oh, indeed you are!' She grinned, recalling their long night of passionate lovemaking. 'Have you been up long?'

He nodded. 'I rose about two hours ago, and went out for a long walk. This countryside is very beautiful. Especially early in the morning, when the fields are still covered in dew.'

As he'd been speaking she'd realised that he was wearing the formal clothes which he'd worn on his arrival. So, this was it, she told herself, a hard lump suddenly forming in her stomach. He was obviously about to bid her farewell before starting on his journey back to Spain.

'It looks as though you're about to drive back to London,' she said as lightly as she could, determined not to spoil their last few moments together.

'Yes, you're quite right, I am,' he agreed, taking a small packet out of his jacket pocket and placing it in her hands before rising to his feet and walking over to gaze out of the window.

'What's this? A leaving present?' she asked, undoing the wrapping paper to disclose a large, square box.

'It's just a little thing I picked up for you yesterday,' he murmured, turning his dark head towards her and watching as she opened the box to reveal a wide gold bracelet studded with diamonds and pearls.

'Oh... Antonio! *It's lovely!*' she gasped, unable to prevent a small tear from trickling down her cheek.

'I'm sorry,' she muttered. 'I meant to be so cool and sophisticated. But…but it's no good. I really *am* going to miss you. So much!' She sniffed, quickly raising a hand to brush the tears from her eyes.

'Ah, my darling! There is no need for you to weep,' he protested, striding quickly across the carpet and removing the tray before sitting down on the bed beside her. 'I really have no choice but to fly back to Spain first thing tomorrow morning,' he added, gently drying her eyes with his large pocket handkerchief before taking hold of her hands and clasping them firmly within his own.

'Yes, I know,' she muttered.

'I have been troubled as how best to handle this situation between us,' he told her. 'However, after much thought this morning, I realised it was important to speak frankly to you now—rather than leave matters until I returned home to Spain. And, since I know my own heart, since I know that I wish to marry you, I realised I must say so, before I leave this country.'

'*M-marry me…?*' She raised her head to stare at him in astonishment.

'But, yes—of course!' He smiled down at her. 'How can you doubt it? Surely you must have understood my feelings for you?'

'But…but I really had no idea… I mean, it never occurred to me!' she exclaimed helplessly, before struggling to pull herself together. 'I'm sorry, but you've taken me completely by surprise,' she told him, feeling distinctly light-headed. 'Why? Why do you want to marry me?'

He gave a shrug of his broad shoulders. 'How can one answer such a question? There are so many reasons. Some very natural, practical ones, of course. For instance, it is important to me that we shall have much in common. Especially since our families have worked and traded together for so many years. Also, I am now the head of my family, and responsible for their financial welfare. So, it is clearly time that I settled down. There are other, more personal reasons, of course.'

'Such as…?' she queried breathlessly, almost certain that she must be in the middle of a dream and going to wake up to hard, cold reality at any minute.

'Well, now…' He paused his dark eyes gleaming with laughter as he stared down at her dazed expression. 'Maybe it is because I find you totally enchanting? Or possibly because we share the same sense of humour? Or…yes—I have it! Because you are the only woman I know who does *not* like to go shopping.'

'Oh—Antonio!' she groaned impatiently. '*Do* be serious for a moment—or I really will have hysterics. Those are obviously *not* good enough reasons why either of us should want to get married. What about love?'

'Ah, *querida*…my lovely, dearest Gina,' he breathed thickly, pulling her into his arms and burying his face in her long fragrant hair. 'You must have seen…you must surely know that I am in love with you? Yes, of course…' he added quickly as she stirred restlessly in his arms, 'I know that it must seem strange to suddenly see someone—after *such* a long length of time—and to realise that you have *always* have been in love with them. But it is so. Right from the first moment I looked up into your lovely face, when I mistakenly thought I was rescuing you from a dangerously bolting horse. It was like…' He paused for a moment, searching for the right words. 'I can only say that it was like a sudden bolt of lightning! I just *knew*…knew with all my heart and soul…that you were the woman with whom I wished to spend the rest of my life.'

Almost fainting with happiness, Gina couldn't say anything for a moment, and then she felt his hands tightening on her shoulders as he pressed her back against the pillows, gazing searchingly into her dazed blue eyes.

'And you, my lovely Gina? You are in love with me, too? *Sí?*'

'Well...yes...yes, I am,' she muttered, feeling her heart turning over as he pressed tender, feather-light kisses on her upturned face.

'But...but we have only spent a very few days together,' she reminded him breathlessly. 'And, while I really *do* love you very much, I really hadn't thought of marriage. It's such a big step. Not something to take lightly, or...'

'Ah, my dearest,' he murmured, his lips moving softly over her own. 'Surely you want me in your bed every night?'

'Oh, Antonio...*of course* I do...' she whispered, winding her slim arms about his neck and fervently responding to the sweet seduction of his warm mouth as he firmly possessed her lips, trembling beneath the tender, caressing touch of his hands on her body.

'So—you will accept my proposal of marriage?' he demanded, raising his dark head to stare intently down at the girl lying dazed in his arms.

'Yes...' She gave a breathless laugh. 'If you keep on kissing me like that—how could I possibly refuse?'

'*Bueno!*' He grinned. 'So, we will be married—and as soon as possible!'

wish to be responsible for parting him to London.
They agreed — exhausted that he is surely.

'It's going to look a funeral since when he hears,
from you and ...'

Bill Augustin from ...ppeared ... and the ...don
...

CHAPTER FIVE

AND so I married him!' Gina wrote, pausing to gaze out over the deep blue sea, and wondering just how much more she could squeeze on to the postcard which she was sending to an old girlfriend.

Everything had happened so swiftly that she was now having to write to many of her friends and acquaintances telling them she was now a married woman. A *very* happily married woman, she told herself with a grin, leaning back on her chair on the large balcony outside their bedroom in this glamorous hotel in the Canary Islands.

The choice of their honeymoon destination had been Antonio's. He, as she might have guessed, had wanted to combine their private time together with visits to some notable *bodegas* in Las Palmas and Tenerife. And, while she was utterly and blissfully content in her new married life, she still regarded her wedding as being one of the happiest days of her life.

Antonio, frantically working against time to bring some order and method to the old-fashioned Bodega Ramirez in Jerez before the grapes were due to be harvested, had left all the arrangements to her. Although even before returning to London from Suffolk, on the Sunday before his flight back to Spain, they had already decided on a very quiet, family wedding.

'We must think of your grandfather,' Antonio had pointed out. 'He is definitely not well. And I do not want to be responsible for causing him to become more tired or exhausted than he is already.'

'He's going to get a terrific shock when he hears about you and me!' she'd laughed.

But Antonio hadn't appeared to find the situation quite as amusing as she had. In fact, it had almost been as if he was nervous. Clearly he hadn't been looking forward to the meeting with Sir Robert Brandon.

'Don't worry. I'm sure Grandpa will be pleased about us,' she'd told him reassuringly. 'And I'll be there, too, of course.'

'No. These things are best handled man to man. And it is the right way of doing things,' he'd told her firmly. 'After all, my darling, your grandfather is of the old school, *no*? And he will, therefore, expect me to formally ask for your hand in marriage.'

She had no way of knowing exactly what had been said at the meeting between the two men. But, after waiting for some time in the large sitting room of the old house in Pall Mall, she'd been relieved when Antonio had led her into her grandfather's study to find the elderly man almost over the moon with joy.

'I have no doubts about this marriage,' he'd told her with a beaming smile. 'I'm quite certain that he is absolutely the right husband for you. In fact,' he'd added, turning to give Antonio a wink, 'I definitely couldn't have chosen a better man myself!'

But, clearly fearing they might tire the old gentleman, Antonio had announced that he was taking his new fiancée out to dinner. Where they'd quickly and happily decided on the sort of low-key wedding they both preferred, setting a date three weeks ahead.

'I must buy you a proper engagement ring,' Antonio had told her. 'I would obviously like to have done so in Ipswich. But it seemed premature—since I hadn't yet asked you to marry me. I also felt that you would like to be involved in choosing your own ring,' he'd added, taking her hand in his before lifting it to his lips.

'Which is why,' he'd continued, pressing light kisses on her quivering fingers, 'I only felt able to give you that bracelet. I wanted you to have something from me—even if you turned down my proposal.'

Oh, Antonio!' she'd murmured, gazing starry-eyed at the diamond- and pearl-studded bracelet on her wrist. 'It's *beautiful*! And really, you know, there's no need to have an engagement ring. We are going to be married in three weeks' time, after all.'

'Nevertheless, I will be giving you a ring,' he'd told her firmly. 'But can you make all the arrangements in such a short space of time?' he'd queried with a slight frown. 'I'm sorry to leave everything to you, but I have no choice but to get back to Jerez as soon as possible.'

'*No problema!*' She'd grinned, making a mental note to organise a special marriage licence first thing on Monday morning.

It had been a frantic three weeks, of course. After consulting her grandfather, Gina had immediately promoted the head salesman at the branch office in Suffolk to take over her job as manager. She had then seemed to spend the rest of the time before her wedding driving up and down the motorway, trying to help and support her successor in Ipswich as well as making arrangements for the wedding in London.

All of which had meant that there'd been no time to plan exactly where she and Antonio were going to live after they were married. But, as she'd pointed out

in one of their many phone calls, his family owned a
great deal of property in and around Jerez. So it would
probably be best to leave that decision until after the
wedding.

And so, on a warm Saturday afternoon—wearing a
simply three-quarter length dress of pale ivory chiffon,
with a headband of white rosebuds and deep green
leaves, over her long blonde hair—she had been married to the man whom she loved with all her heart.

It had been a quiet, simple ceremony, with few
guests. Unfortunately neither of Antonio's sisters had
been present—Isabella because she was expecting another baby, and had been unable to fly over for the
wedding, and Roxana had already been committed to
attending an important première that evening in
Barcelona. But Antonio's brother-in-law, Jaime, had
been there, as best man. And besides her grandfather,
together with many of his staff from the shop, Gina
had also been warmed by the presence of her beloved
godmother, Joyce Frazer, who'd insisted on making
all arrangements for the simple reception in the large
rooms of the family house in Pall Mall.

But they'd really had no need of anyone else as
they'd looked deeply into each other's eyes while taking their vows.

And now, after a wonderful week alone together,
they were flying to Cadiz early tomorrow morning, for
a grand family reunion, organised by Antonio's grandmother, to welcome his new bride. After which she
and her new husband would be flying to California,
where Antonio had arranged some important meetings
with several prominent wine-makers in the Napa
Valley.

Quite honestly, Gina told herself now, leaning over

the balcony and smiling down at her new husband, sipping coffee as he read the morning newspaper, she had to be—without a shadow of doubt—the luckiest woman in the world!

'The landscape doesn't seem to have changed at all since I was last here,' she said the next day, gazing out of the window of the car as Antonio drove them along the road leading to Jerez de la Fontera. There were still the same huge acres of vines, marching row upon row across the white, chalky soil on either side of the road. And the mountain range in the distance appeared wreathed in the same misty grey and pale lilac colours that she remembered so well.

The family hadn't really changed, either. Antonio's old grandmother, Doña Ramirez, was perhaps just a little more stooped. But she was still able to enfold her grandson's bride firmly in her arms.

'*Hermosa!* So pretty!' she murmured, giving Gina a smacking kiss on both cheeks before patting the girl's slim stomach and telling her there was no time to be lost in producing a great-grandson to carry on the family name.

'For heaven's sake, Abuela! Give the poor girl a chance to get used to married life,' a well-known voice called out from the crowd, and Roxana laughingly ran forward to give her old friend a large hug.

'*Hola*, Gina! You haven't changed a bit.' The Spanish girl grinned up at her. 'Except to grow taller, of course.'

'Well...you've *definitely* changed,' Gina said astounded to find herself looking down at a girl she hardly recognised.

Instead of the plump, rather plain eighteen year old

whom she remembered, Roxana was now a very slim, highly glamorous and clearly ultra-sophisticated woman, dressed in the height of fashion. Only the same infectious cheeky grin and the large sparkling dark eyes hadn't changed over the past eight years.

'Heavens! You look so smart,' Gina exclaimed. 'Just like a film star.'

'Well—that's what I am. Or very nearly,' Roxana laughed. 'Didn't my brother tell you? I've just signed my first contract to appear in a film. It's only a small, low-budget movie, of course, but...'

'Oh, my goodness—how exciting!' Gina beamed at her. 'You must tell me all about it, and...'

'She can do that later.' Antonio grinned, firmly taking her arm and introducing his new bride to the other members of the family, whom she hadn't met before. And also some that she had.

'You may remember Carlotta Perez?' he murmured, leading her up to an outstandingly beautiful, svelte woman whom she had no problem in recalling from her visit eight years ago.

She was a distant cousin of Antonio's, and Carlotta and Gina had taken an instantaneous mutual dislike to one another. And their feelings had not changed during the remainder of the time Gina had stayed with Roxana's family before returning to England.

Their instinctive antipathy to one another had not been helped by Carlotta, who'd constantly referred to the younger girl as 'that boring little English mouse'. While Gina, for her part, had been wildly jealous of the older, highly glamorous and sophisticated Spanish girl, who'd clearly been mad about Antonio.

That was all a long time ago, of course. However, if she'd hoped that the girl, whom she'd never liked, might have run to fat, or lost her attraction, Gina was doomed to disappointment. Because, unfortunately, Carlotta still looked absolutely stunning!

The sculptured perfection of her face, the warm golden skin and midnight-black hair arranged in loose curls—not to mention her deliciously rounded, full-breasted figure, which seemed to have been poured into that skin-tight black silk dress—almost took Gina's breath away.

'*Hola…*' Carlotta murmured, putting out a languid hand, her glinting black eyes skimming disdainfully over Gina's simple summer dress, clearly coming to the conclusion that Antonio's new bride appeared to be the same boring English girl whom she'd met all those years ago.

Suddenly feeling highly depressed, Gina was relieved to have her attention distracted by the late arrival of Isabella and her husband, together with their small daughters. And clearly Doña Ramirez had been waiting for them. Because she soon called everyone to come and have lunch out on the large patio behind the house, which was shielded from the hot midday sun by the shady overhead trellis of vine leaves.

'It's been so wonderful to meet all the family again,' Gina told her old friend Roxana some hours later as they sat upstairs in one of the large spare bedrooms, freshening themselves up after the long, leisurely lunch.

'And it's great to meet you again, too.' Her old friend laughed. 'Gina hasn't changed at all, has she?' she added, turning to Carlotta, who was sitting at the dressing table repairing her make-up.

'No, you're right—she hasn't,' the other girl murmured, appearing totally absorbed in applying another thick coat of mascara to her long black eyelashes.

Gina struggled to keep a straight face as Roxana grimaced and rolled her eyes. Clearly her new sister-in-law still harboured feelings of dislike for her older cousin. Which wasn't surprising when she recalled how Carlotta had always treated the younger girl, with much the same disdain and condescension as she had used towards Gina.

'Well, Señora Ramirez—how does it feel to be an old married lady?' Roxana asked with a grin. 'I hope Antonio is being a good husband!'

'Oh, yes, he is!' Gina gave her a broad smile. 'Everything seemed to happen in a terrific rush, of course. But Antonio is just…well, he's just *wonderful*! He makes me very happy,' she added, her cheeks flushing as Carlotta gave a harsh bark of laughter.

'I should hope he *does* make you happy,' the other woman told her scornfully. 'Your grandfather is certainly paying enough for him—that's for sure!'

Gina frowned at her, before turning to Roxana. 'What on earth's she talking about?'

'*Poof! Carlotta—estúpida!*' her friend said with a quick shrug of her slim shoulders. 'Take no notice of her.'

'Oh-ho! If anyone in this room is *stupid* it is your friend the English Mouse,' Carlotta flashed back, swinging around on the stool and scowling at Roxana. 'How can she be so naïve? Does she *really* think that Antonio would have even *looked* at her if she wasn't the heiress to her oh-so-rich grandfather?'

'That's utterly ridiculous!' Gina snapped.

'Really?' Carlotta drawled spitefully. 'Then why don't you ask Roxana here—or any other member of the family, for that matter—just *why* Uncle Emilio is telling anyone who'll listen that he and Sir Robert Brandon have arranged this marriage?'

'What rubbish!' Gina gave an angry laugh. 'My grandfather had absolutely nothing to do with my marriage to Antonio.'

'Uncle Emilio is a very sick old man,' Roxana said, immediately springing to the defence of her old schoolfriend. 'Of course he's very pleased about Antonio's marriage. Why shouldn't he be?'

Turning to Gina, she added, 'Take no notice of Carlotta. She's always been spiteful, and very, *very* stupid.'

'Ah-ha!' Carlotta exclaimed, before throwing back her lovely head and giving a shrill ripple of caustic laughter. 'You keep saying that I am stupid—but what about this silly English friend of yours? Hasn't she ever heard of a marriage of convenience?' she continued scathingly. 'Doesn't she realise that if plain, boring little rich girls want a handsome, virile husband they have to *buy* him, one way or another!'

'That's quite enough of your nonsense!' Roxana snapped, jumping to her feet and then yelling loudly at the other girl in Spanish.

As the two of them vigorously exchanged insults in their native language, Gina stood frozen, as if turned to a pillar of stone as she tried to understand what Carlotta had been saying.

A marriage of convenience? What on earth did that mean in relation to her and Antonio? And that foul remark about her grandfather 'paying' for Antonio was totally ridiculous. In fact it was utterly laughable. Because that proud Spaniard Antonio Ramirez was the very *last* man to allow himself to be bought—or be forced to do anything he didn't want to.

'You're just green with jealousy,' Roxana was now yelling angrily at Carlotta in English. 'You've *always* wanted Antonio. And you can't bear the fact that he's fallen in love with Gina and married her instead! In fact, if you ask me...' she was adding, when there was a loud knock at the door.

An immediate silence fell on the room as the two Spanish girls stopped screaming at one another and turned expectantly to face the door.

'Come on!' Roxana's eldest sister Isabella said, putting her head into the room. 'Everyone's downstairs waiting for you. Antonio's organised a tour of the Bodega Ramirez, for the family to inspect some of the new alterations he's been making. So hurry up—or we'll be leaving you behind!' she said, before disappearing from sight.

The atmosphere in the bedroom after Isabella had left was so tense, Gina thought, that you cold practically cut it with a knife. But Carlotta had made her life a misery when she'd been staying with Roxana's family eight years ago. And she sure as hell wasn't going to allow it to happen again.

'I...er...I think I'll just go and get my handbag downstairs,' Roxana muttered, after one quick glance at the grim determination etched on Gina's face.

'OK—let's get this thing sorted out once and for all,' Gina grated angrily as the door closed behind her old schoolfriend.

'Goodness knows you and I have never particularly liked each other, Carlotta. And I have no idea of what is prompting you to make these nasty, snide remarks. But, for your information, I can tell you that Antonio

and I are *very* happily married. And if you don't like
that fact—well, that's just too bad, isn't it?'

However, far from looking abashed, or ashamed of
her behaviour, Carlotta merely gave Gina a feline, cat-
like smile in the mirror as she resumed painting her
lips in a deep crimson.

'Relax! There's no need to sound so upset, Gina,'
she murmured. 'As far as I can see your marriage
sounds like a very sensible business arrangement. And
of course you're happy with Antonio. Why shouldn't
you be? As we both know, he's a fantastic lover. So
you're lucky to have him in your bed—for the time
being, anyway!'

'I've never heard such a horrid mass of poisonous
innuendo and spitefulness in all my life!' Gina ground
out angrily. 'I reckon Roxana is absolutely right.
You've always been mad about Antonio. And you just
can't accept the fact that he prefers me to you.'

The other girl shrugged her slim, elegant shoulders.
'If that's what you want to believe keep on living in
that happy little dream, Gina,' she sneered. 'But if you
want to know the truth…why not ask Uncle Emilio?
After all, he's bursting with pride, telling everyone just
how clever he's been in arranging Antonio's marriage.
I'm sure he'll be able to fill you in concerning the
small print of the marriage contract!'

'I've never heard such rubbish!' Gina retorted,
quickly snatching up her handbag and preparing to
leave the room. 'There is no ''marriage contract'', as
you call it. Besides, as far as your Uncle Emilio is
concerned, I haven't seen the man for the past eight
years.

'Incidentally,' she added walking away determinedly towards the door, 'I suggest that you keep

well away from my husband. Neither of us would wish to have any contact with someone like you—who so obviously enjoys spreading poison wherever she goes.'

'I don't see how I *can* keep away from your husband,' Carlotta drawled as Gina opened the door. 'Haven't you heard about my new job?'

'What new job?' Gina queried tersely.

'Not having been in touch with the family for so long, you obviously don't know that, very far from being stupid, I'm a first-rate business woman,' Carlotta told her, brushing some flecks of invisible dust from the sleeve of her tight black dress. 'Which is why your dear husband has just appointed me as the head of his new accounts department. And with so many other pressures on him at the moment, I *really* don't think that darling Antonio will be in any hurry to lose me!' she added with a tinkling laugh as she turned back to examine her face in the mirror.

Glaring at the other woman for a moment, Gina realised that there was nothing to be gained by continuing to trade insults with this truly awful woman. Unfortunately slamming the door very loudly behind her did little to soothe her turbulent emotions.

However, as she ran down the stairs to join the rest of the party assembling outside on the forecourt of the old house, her mind was still in a total whirl. Nothing that awful girl Carlotta said had made any sense. Although she'd managed to draw blood with some of those poisonous darts, Gina reminded herself grimly.

If Carlotta *had* always wanted Antonio, it sounded as though she'd now managed to cleverly manoeuvre herself into a position where she'd been able to see him practically every day. Nor had Gina missed

Carlotta's throwaway line about the fact that she and
Antonio had been lovers.

Well...there was nothing that she could do about
that, Gina told herself firmly. She was now married to
Antonio, and loved him with all her heart. Besides,
whatever had happened in the past, it had nothing to
do with their present happiness.

As for all that nonsense about poor old Uncle
Emilio? Well, that was what it was—just nonsense.

'The Ramirez family originally came from the North
of Spain in the eighteenth century. They entered the
wine trade in 1795, when José Ramirez inherited a
sherry business from his father-in-law.'

As the general manager of the Bodega Ramirez
paused, consulting his notes before launching himself
yet again on the history of the Ramirez family and
their world-famous wines, Gina was finding it difficult
to concentrate. First there'd been the dreadful confrontation with Carlotta Perez. And then, the very disturbing conversation with old Uncle Emilio.

She'd known, of course, that Antonio's uncle had
recently been forced to hand over the reins of the business—primarily because of his ill health and increasing age. However, since their arrival here at the family
house today, she hadn't been given the opportunity to
do more than greet the elderly gentleman. So that
might have been why she'd been chosen to join him
in his chauffeur-driven limousine, which had been spe-
cially constructed to take his wheelchair.

'I am so happy...*very* happy, that you and my
nephew have become married. It is good, *no*?' he'd
told her in heavily accented, hesitant English. 'I re-

member you, Gina. So many years ago. Such a pretty young girl.'

He had beamed happily at the young woman sitting beside him.

'I, too, am happy,' she'd said, striving to keep the conversation as simple as possible, since she was well aware of the fact that, with virtually no command of the Spanish language, she was going to have to take lessons straight away. And it was also clear that Antonio's uncle spoke very little English.

'Yes...it is good. As I said to your *abuelo*—your grandfather—we must make this marriage. Antonio needs a good wife, and a rich one, eh!' He'd chuckled, giving her a slight dig in the ribs. 'And so we planned it all. We two old men. But we are still clever, *no*?' He'd given another heavy, throaty chuckle.

'I don't quite understand...' Gina had muttered, his heavy accent making it difficult to comprehend what the old man was saying.

'Antonio is a good man. I tell him, "You must get married. You need a nice girl, with a good dowry." And see...he has now married you. Yes, Antonio is a good man. He does as he is told. And Don Roberto...he tells me he is pleased with this marriage.' He had turned to smile at her again.

'My grandfather?' Gina had queried, her brain in a whirl.

'*Sí*...Don Roberto, he says you are a good girl. And this is a good marriage for you. So send me Antonio, he says—and I will see him marry my Gina!'

The old man had turned to beam at the pretty woman whom his nephew had just taken as a wife. Everything had worked out as he and Don Roberto had planned. Now it only remained for the young couple to produce a son and heir. Which would complete his happiness and ensure that the Bodega Ramirez would be owned and run by future generations of the family.

'Our two families…they are now like that,' he'd said, putting his two hands together as the vehicle came to a halt outside a large building in one of the squares in the centre of Jerez.

'And so Don Roberto tells me not to worry,' the old man had continued. 'He says, if Antonio marry you, he will make sure he has plenty money for the Bodega. It is good, *no*?' he'd added, as the chauffeur had come around to open the door and help the old gentleman out of the car.

'The company has passed down through six generations of the Ramirez family. It is today one of only a handful of independent sherry producers, who…'

As the general manager's voice droned on, Gina was still trying to make sense of what Antonio's uncle had been saying.

According to the old man, it sounded as though he seemed to think that he and her grandfather had somehow conspired to bring about the marriage between herself and Antonio. Which was obviously ridiculous. As was that nonsense—if she's understood the old man correctly—about her grandfather giving money to Antonio for the *bodega*—the wine-making plant. Because he wouldn't have done anything like that without telling her, she assured herself firmly. All the same…

Gina gave a slight start as she became aware of her husband suddenly standing behind her.

Lowering his dark head, he murmured quietly in her ear, 'This talk is very boring, *no*? However, we have a very fine old ''Cathedral Cellar'', which I think you will find more interesting,' he added, taking hold of her hand and quietly leading her from the room.

Following Antonio along the twisting corridors and passages of the old building, Gina learned that it had once been the large headquarters of a West Indian merchant who'd made a fortune doing business with the American colonies in the eighteenth century. However, nowadays it was used by the Ramirez family as a *bodega*, for the production, storage and sale of their world-famous sherries.

Eventually it seemed that they had reached their destination, as Antonio opened a large old oak door, switching on the light and leading her carefully down some ancient, wide stone steps.

Gina could see immediately why the cellar had been called a 'cathedral'. In fact, she'd never seen such a vast, huge space devoted solely to barrel upon barrel of wine. Gazing up at the very high and steep double-pitched roof supported by tall pillars and ornate arches, she could only marvel at the time it must have taken to construct such a huge building.

'This was built, of course, at the end of the eighteenth century. It produces a special climatic condition for our *fino* wines...but I won't bore you with too much technology!' Antonio told her with a grin, his voice echoing weirdly in the enormous space. 'However, it is magnificent, *no*?'

Gina nodded. Yes, it was truly amazing. But she couldn't seem to concentrate on the sight in front of her. Not when her mind now seemed to be filled with so many unanswered questions.

'Are you all right?' Antonio queried, gazing at her

with concern. 'You're looking a bit pale. I hope nothing you ate at lunch has upset you.'

She shook her head. 'No, I'm fine. It's just…well, I've had two rather upsetting conversations this afternoon. First with Carlotta, then with your uncle. And, to tell you the truth, I don't quite understand what's going on….'

'Which is—what?' he asked. And, when she didn't immediately reply, he added, 'If you have a problem, Gina, I think that you'd better tell me about it, hmm?'

'It seems our marriage is the problem,' she declared, looking him straight in the eye. 'Carlotta and I have never been friends. So it's not surprising that I didn't take any notice when she claimed that you and I have entered into a marriage of convenience. But then I had a very strange conversation with your uncle.'

'So? What did my uncle say?' Antonio demanded, frowning down at his wife, who appeared unusually disturbed and almost unhappy.

'Quite frankly, your uncle's English isn't very good. Almost as non-existent as my Spanish,' she told him. 'But, from what I could make out, he seemed to be claiming that he and my grandfather had arranged our marriage.'

'But that's ridiculous—as well you must know!' Antonio laughed.

Gina shrugged. 'Well, according to your uncle, he told you to get married to a rich girl and seems very pleased that you've apparently followed his instructions. However, he also seems to have been in touch with my grandfather. And, while I still can't quite work out the finer details of their arrangement, there definitely seems to be the question of some money from my grandfather for your family company flying around.'

'Nonsense!'

'On top of which,' she continued, despite his interjection, 'I had to put up with Carlotta—who appears to be convinced that you only married me because my grandfather had paid you to do so. An allegation which, I must admit, I find very upsetting.'

'I've never heard such a farrago of utter silliness!' Antonio told her firmly. 'And you should not listen to such things either.'

'Nevertheless, it seems that there *is* something going on, and I want to get to the bottom of it, right now,' she told him stubbornly. 'Just how much of what your uncle told me is true? Did he tell you to go and find a rich girl with a large dowry?'

'That is all totally absurd!' Antonio growled, brushing a hand angrily through his dark hair. 'Yes, my uncle did want me to get married and settle down. But surely it's natural for an old man to feel that way? The idea that I would simply do as he told me is utterly ludicrous.'

'OK…but what about *my* grandfather? Why are Carlotta and your uncle both claiming that you married me simply because I'm heiress to my grandfather's fortune? They must have got the information from somewhere—right? Besides, I know you saw him before you came up to Suffolk, and…'

'How can you say such things?' Antonio demanded angrily.

'But Carlotta and your uncle both seem to believe…' Gina's voice died away, her slim body shivering with both tension and the chilly atmosphere within the enormous stone-walled cellar.

'I don't *know* what Carlotta said. How could I? I wasn't there. While she's a good business woman, in every other aspect she's a flawed personality,' he ground out furiously. 'And, as you've seen, my uncle is both old and infirm.

'However, I can categorically deny that I married you for any reason other than the fact that I wished to do so,' he added, clearly struggling to control his fiery Spanish temper. 'And that you should doubt me...that you should not trust and believe what I say...I find that unforgivable, Gina!'

Opening her mouth to tell him that she was really very sorry for having allowed herself to be wound up by Carlotta, she was prevented from doing so by a sudden shout from the top of the stone stairs behind them.

'Antonio! There you are...' his brother-in-law Jaime called out.

'Not now!' Antonio yelled back impatiently. 'I will see you later.'

'No! It is *very* important that I talk to you. *Immediately!*' Jaime insisted.

With a heavy sigh, Antonio turned and began walking rapidly towards the stone steps, beckoning Gina to follow him. But, though she trailed slowly behind him, by the time she reached the top of the steps both he and his brother-in-law seemed to have disappeared.

Still feeling shattered at the first major quarrel with her husband, and deeply ashamed of having wrongly accused him of such dreadful behaviour, she wandered slowly back down the corridors towards the main reception area of the *bodega*.

But she hadn't gone very far before Antonio suddenly appeared, quickly taking her arm and leading her out of the building by a side door, towards his car. He was looking very stern. His face was set in such harsh lines that she suddenly felt deeply apprehensive.

'What's wrong?' she asked, as he silently held open the passenger door of his car.

'I am taking you home, Gina,' he said quietly. 'I need to talk to you. And with the *bodega* full of friends and relatives, I think we'll have more peace and quiet at home.'

It was a short journey, and yet by the time they arrived back at the family house Gina felt totally strung up with tension. What on earth had possessed her? How *could* she have accused her darling husband of marrying her for money?

But she wasn't given any time to dwell on the subject as Antonio brought the car to a halt outside the house. Quickly taking hold of her arm, he led her firmly in through the front door, past the tearful, clearly distressed figure of his grandmother, and swiftly on down the corridor to a door at the far end, leading on to the large garden behind the house.

'For heaven's sakes!' she gasped, as he guided her towards a bench beneath one of the flowering trees. 'What's going on? I'm really…*really* sorry I said all those things, Antonio,' she pleaded, almost tearfully. 'I honestly didn't mean to accuse you…I really didn't know what I was saying. I do hope that…'

'Hush, *querida*,' he murmured, sitting down on the bench beside her before putting his arms around her trembling figure.

'The fact is, my darling, I…I'm afraid that I have some bad news for you,' he murmured, pressing his face into her hair for a moment. 'There has just been a phone call from your godmother. To say that…that your grandfather was rushed to hospital this morning, following a very serious heart attack. And I fear he is not expected to survive for more than a few hours at the most.'

As she gave a low cry, her slim figure trembling, he gently rocked her in his arms. 'It is a terrible shock for you, *no*?' he told her softly. 'But we will catch the first plane to England. All may yet be well with your grandfather. Modern science...modern medicine can work wonders. All may yet be well.'

But Gina's brain seemed frozen. The news was, of course, an awful blow. And, coming on top of that deeply upsetting quarrel with Antonio, it seemed a long time before the mists began to clear in her brain.

However, as she sat enfolded in the warmth of her beloved husband's arms, she gradually realised that, deep in her subconscious, she must have known that she would have to face the news of her grandfather's demise at some point within the foreseeable future. She was going to miss him...desperately. But, as he'd so often said, he'd had a long life, full of enjoyment and pleasure.

'Come...' Antonio said at last, his voice seeming to come from a long way off as he placed a hand gently beneath her chin, lifting her tear-stained face towards him.

'Come, my darling,' he said quietly, taking a large handkerchief from his pocket and gently drying her tears. 'I think we must pack and leave as soon as possible. I will make arrangements for us to catch the next plane to London, yes?'

CHAPTER SIX

GINA knew that she would never forget that nightmare journey back to England.

The long, tiring flight from Spain and their frantic drive from the airport proved to be of no avail. By the time she and Antonio reached the hospital she learned that her grandfather had died some hours before, and that she would never have the opportunity to say good-bye to him.

Eventually arriving home at the large old house in Pall Mall, she was comforted by the warm welcome and sympathy extended by her grandfather's manservant, Harold Preston. He, together with his wife Anna—who, for as long as Gina could remember, had reined supreme in the kitchen—did their best to ensure that she had as few problems to cope with as possible.

Although what she would have done without Antonio by her side, Gina had absolutely no idea.

It was a shock to discover that following a death in the family there should be so much paperwork, so many forms to fill in and so many arrangements to make concerning the funeral.

After some discussion, she and Antonio agreed that it would probably be best if they held a quiet, private funeral for her grandfather, to be followed by a large and formal memorial service.

'He was an important man,' Antonio pointed out. 'Which means there will be many of his old friends and acquaintances, as well as many colleagues in the wine trade, who will wish to pay their respects. So, would you like me to ask his secretary to compile a list of…how do you say it here in England?…''the great and the good''?'

'Oh, yes—thank you!' Gina breathed a heavy sigh of relief. 'There are so many letters of condolence to answer. And I haven't a clue about some of Grandpa's old friends. I'd hate to be guilty of not sending out invitations to those who might have been important in his life.'

When it began raining on the day of the funeral, it somehow seemed appropriate, Gina told herself, arriving at the ancient church where she and Antonio had been married only a few weeks ago. And, although it was a desperately sad occasion, she felt immeasurably strengthened to have Antonio's tall, broad-shouldered figure standing closely by her side, firmly holding her hand within his own firm clasp.

Later that evening, as they sat on the sofa in her grandfather's study—she couldn't yet face the huge, icily formal drawing room upstairs, on the first floor— she savoured the relief of being able to place her head on Antonio's broad, comforting shoulder as they talked quietly together about the events of the day.

'Unfortunately, my darling,' he said at last, 'I'm afraid that I will have to leave you for some days, since I really cannot afford to cancel my trip to California. As you know, some of the Napa Valley wine-growers have kindly agreed to show me around their vineyards. And, since the Americans are leaders in the use of modern technology, it is vitally important for me to see what they are doing—and if it can be applied to my own business.'

'Yes, of course you must go,' she said, before adding with a sigh, 'I wish I could come with you.'

'Umm…I wish you could be there with me, too,' he said, pressing a quick kiss on her brow. 'But Sir Robert's secretary seems to have all the arrangements here well in hand. And I will definitely be back to support you at the memorial service.'

'I must say that's a relief. I hardly recognise any of the names on this list, which has been drawn up by Grandpa's secretary. And I'm *really* going to need you by my side when I have to meet and greet all these people.'

'There's no need to worry—I'll be there. And in any case, my darling, there's that meeting tomorrow with your family lawyer,' he pointed out. 'If, as seems likely, you have inherited the whole of your grandfather's business, you'll be far too busy to have any time to miss me.'

It had been a wrench to wave her new husband goodbye earlier that morning, Gina told herself the next day, as the taxi dropped her off outside the large, anonymous-looking building in the City of London. She'd never had any dealings with her grandfather's firm of lawyers, and she wasn't quite sure what was likely to happen regarding his will.

However, in the event, she found herself being shown into a large, thoroughly modern office, and being greeted with a hearty handshake by a large, rather avuncular-looking middle-aged man.

'As I believe you already know, Sir Robert had always intended you to be his sole heiress,' the lawyer said, after having sat her down comfortably in front of his desk and provided a soothing cup of coffee.

'There are one or two private bequests, such as those to his servants, of course. But in all other respects you are now the sole proprietor of Brandon's of Pall Mall.'

As she sat there, wondering what she was supposed to say or do at this point, the lawyer continued, 'I'm pleased to say that your grandfather's estate is remarkably free of any encumbrances. Other than the codicil which he recently added to his will, of course. In fact, Mrs...er...Señora Ramirez—' he gave her a beaming smile '—it would seem that you are now a very, *very* wealthy woman.'

'A codicil?' she murmured with a slight frown.

The lawyer nodded. 'I'm sure I don't need to bore you with all the legal jargon,' he said, adjusting the papers on the desk in front of him. 'Your grandfather came to see me, just over a month ago, and asked me to draw up this codicil—a legal addition to his main Will and Testament. It stated that when the proposed marriage between yourself and your fiancé took place, Señor Don Antonio Ramirez would receive a certain amount of money, for his own sole use.'

The lawyer paused, adjusting his glasses as he peered down at the document in front of him.

'Sir Robert also added a comment to the effect that he hoped Señor Don Antonio Ramirez would use the bequest to generally improve and modernise his wine-making business in Spain.'

Gina gazed at him steadily for a moment. 'When you say "a certain amount of money"—just how much are we talking about?'

Consulting the paper again, the lawyer mentioned a sum which fairly took Gina's breath away.

'That…that's a really *enormous* amount of money!' she exclaimed.

But the solicitor merely shrugged his shoulders. 'It is one which the estate can well afford. In fact, I recall your grandfather mentioning that, since you were marrying Don Antonio, he regarded it as a very good investment.'

Returning to the large, empty house, and pacing up and down her grandfather's study, Gina tried to come to terms with the full impact of what she'd just learned. Because, whichever way she looked at it, it was now clear that her grandfather and Antonio *had* come to some sort of arrangement. The final proof of the bargain they'd obviously made between them being the date when the codicil had been drawn up—the day immediately after those four romantic days in Suffolk when Antonio—having asked her to marry him and gained her grandfather's approval of their marriage—had flown back to Spain.

Everything Carlotta Perez had said—and old Uncle Emilio, for that matter—now fell neatly into place. Indeed, it didn't need a very high IQ to work out *exactly* what had happened over that long hot weekend just over a month ago.

To begin with, there was the fact that Antonio had clearly been under pressure from his uncle to get married. And not just to find himself a wife—but a rich one, too. And it also seemed highly likely, if she'd understood his uncle correctly, that old Emilio and her grandfather had been talking to one another—probably over the phone.

Gina had also been aware that with her grandfather's increasing age and infirmity he'd been worried about what was going to happen to her when she took over the business.

While her grandpa hadn't made too much of a song and dance about it, he *had* occasionally mentioned that he'd have felt a lot more cheerful about leaving her in charge if she'd had the strong arm of a husband to lean on. Leaving Gina in no doubt that he'd hoped she would be married and settled down by the time she came to inherit the business.

So then—clearly in answer to his prayers—Antonio had turned up, looking for his missing consignment of wine.

She knew that he'd spent some time in the office with her grandfather. And *that's* when they must have hatched their plan, she told herself, trembling with rage at the thought of just how stupid she'd been.

And for Antonio, arriving with very little notice to find her not only alone, but, as it turned out, highly vulnerable to his sensual appeal, it must have seemed the opportunity of a lifetime. Which he'd quickly grabbed with both hands. Because he'd already known—*only too well*—that she'd been madly in love with him all those years ago. It must have seemed as easy as falling off a log to charm the socks off such a foolish, naïve woman.

And you had to hand it to him, he was definitely a fast worker! Because it had only taken Antonio three days of wild, passionate sex—during which she'd clearly been out of her mind—to obtain her agreement to their marriage.

And then, with her in tow, he'd dashed back down to London and told her grandfather the good news, arranged a quick wedding, and hurried off back to Spain.

No wonder Uncle Emilio had been as pleased as punch! It seemed as if everyone—apart from herself, of course—had known that, as soon as her frail, elderly grandfather died, Antonio would have enough money to build a whole, brand-new company headquarters, if he wished to.

Oh, God! What an utter, utter fool she'd been. She really *was*, as Carlotta had so bitchily pointed out, now firmly trapped in a marriage of convenience.

Well…it might be 'convenient' for Antonio, but it looked like being one of sheer hell as far as she was concerned.

As the day of the memorial service came closer, it seemed that it was only sheer anger at both her own stupidity—and her husband's despicable behaviour—which kept her going through the unhappy days and wretchedly tortured nights.

Because she hadn't just been an idiot to fall for Antonio's obvious charms. Even now, when she *knew* what a conniving louse the man really was, she couldn't seem to banish him from her heart. There was no lessening of her intense longing for him, or of her almost overwhelming, aching need for the warmly erotic, sensual caress of his hands on her body.

The only fortunate aspect of the whole rotten business had been the fact that, with the awkward time difference between London and California, they'd already agreed not to try and phone one another. Although Gina knew she was going to have to confront Antonio at some point, she couldn't possibly cope with doing so during a transatlantic phone call.

And, underlying all her anger and fury at what had happened, lay the dreadful knowledge that she was now entirely alone in the world.

She had a godmother, and many friends. But no family of her own. No brothers or sisters, no parents, uncles or aunts—absolutely *no one* to whom she could look for love and support during these hard, difficult days. And it was the increasing feelings of utter loneliness which she found so difficult to combat. Loneliness…and the sense of total betrayal by her husband— the one man she'd thought she could trust, and whom she'd loved with all her heart.

Coming down to breakfast on the day of the memorial service, which was due to take place at eleven o'clock that morning, Gina realised that it had been foolish of her to expect Antonio to turn up.

After all—why should he? she asked herself grimly, catching sight of herself in the hall mirror and wincing at the sight of her pale face, emphasised by the sober black dress she was wearing.

Antonio must know that he'd be getting the money he needed to drag that rotten *bodega* of his into the twenty-first century. So there was clearly no point in forcing himself to go through the motions any more. No need to pretend to be a kind, devoted husband…?

Not able to face anything other than a cup of coffee, Gina was feeling totally wound up and tense as she glanced down at her watch.

Ten o'clock. Well, there was only an hour to go— or less, in fact, since the chauffeured limousine would be coming to pick her up in half an hour. An arrangement made by her grandfather's secretary to ensure that she was at the church well in advance of the guests attending the service.

Then, almost shocking in its suddenness, she heard the sound of Antonio's deep voice greeting Harold, and his firm tread as he walked swiftly down the corridor towards the study.

'I'm sorry to be so late, my darling,' he said, tossing his briefcase down on to a nearby chair. 'I've been working flat out, and only just managed to catch the plane to London by the skin of my teeth. How have you been?'

'How have I been?' Gina gave a shrill, high-pitched laugh. 'Oh, I've been *fine*! Absolutely full of the joys of spring!'

'*Que...?*' he muttered with a slight frown.

'Although I must say I paid a very interesting visit to the family lawyer just after you left. And, as I'm sure you know by now, it looks as though you have no need to worry any more about finding the money to improve your wine-making company. Grandfather really kept his word—*didn't he*?' she added grimly.

Antonio shrugged. 'I don't know what you're talking about,' he told her, before turning to smile at Harold, who had entered the room carrying a tray containing a pot of coffee and two cups and saucers.

'This is just what I need. It was a long and very boring flight,' Antonio said, going over to pour himself a large cup of coffee. 'Would you like some, Gina?'

'No, thank you,' she snapped through clenched teeth as Harold closed the door behind him, before sinking quickly down into a nearby chair as she felt her knees beginning to shake uncontrollably.

'I'm sorry to have left you on your own. I hope it hasn't been too much of a strain for you,' Antonio said, turning around and frowning at the stern, tight expression on his wife's pale face. 'Are you all right, *querida*?'

'No, I'm *not* all right,' she snapped tersely, before explaining in detail about her visit to the lawyer, and how the scales had at last fallen from her eyes.

'Really, Gina! I thought that I'd heard the last of this silly nonsense back in Spain,' he retorted with exasperation.

'But not so silly now, it seems!' she snapped.

'I chose to take no notice of such an unbelievably ridiculous story,' he told her grimly, ignoring her interjection. 'Mainly because I assumed that you'd been upset by some malicious remarks from my trouble-making cousin Carlotta.'

'With whom, as she informed me, you've been having an affair. And you probably are *still* sleeping together—for all I know!' Gina ground out furiously.

'*Dios—no!* That woman means *nothing* to me,' he growled back angrily, before loudly and vociferously denying that he had ever, at any time, chosen to marry her for her money.

'How can you think that, Gina? How can you possibly be such a blind, total fool?' he demanded furiously, his fiery Spanish temper by now well out of control. 'Does our marriage mean *nothing* to you? Have you so little trust in me that you would believe such…such palpable untruths?'

But as far as she was concerned the facts were irrefutable. And she had documented evidence to back her up.

'If, as you say, I'm talking complete rubbish, how is it that my grandfather's codicil was signed and dated on that Monday morning, only hours after you'd asked me to marry you and had just flown back to Spain?' she ground out bitterly through gritted teeth, her head

pounding with a vicious headache and feeling as
though it was going to explode at any moment.

'Are you telling me that everything Carlotta Perez
and your uncle Emilio said is a lie? That my grandfather's will is a *fake*?' she continued, in the face of
his grim, ominous silence.

'No, of course I'm not saying that. And if you
choose to believe Carlotta and my uncle that is your
problem. But what I *am* saying is that you are entirely
mistaken about the money which you say has been left
to me by Sir Robert Brandon,' he told her savagely,
pacing furiously up and down the room. 'I knew *nothing* about this whatsoever. I did not ask for it. I did
not expect it.'

'Hah! A likely story!'

'I can only assure you that I have never wanted—
or needed—that money!' he said more quietly, before
throwing himself down into an armchair and thrusting
his hands roughly through his dark hair.

'Oh…right!' She gave a shrill, high-pitched laugh.
'So, as far as *you're* concerned, it's all just an unfortunate coincidence?'

Having by now wound herself up into a paroxysm
of fury, Gina was finding it almost impossible to control herself. Totally possessed by rage and fury, she
walked restlessly back and forth over the study carpet,
cursing him violently under her breath and waving her
hands distractedly in the air.

'Come! This is enough,' he told her sternly, swiftly
rising from his chair and walking over to place his
hands on her shoulders.

'*Don't touch me!*' she yelled, quickly wriggling
away from beneath his grip. 'You can't seriously be-

lieve that I'm going to fall for that charm of yours yet again?'

'You must calm down, Gina. All this anger is not achieving anything.'

'Well—at least we're facing the truth of the situation at last!' she exclaimed bitterly. 'Because it's all clear to me now. I was such a fool, wasn't I? That silly young schoolgirl with her brain full of equally silly fantasies. She'd fallen madly in love with you once. So why not again, huh?'

'Please, Gina—this is madness! For God's sake, calm down!'

'And I was so easy to manipulate,' she continued, so consumed by anger and pain that she barely heard him. 'Did you have fun working it out with my grandfather? But, yes, of course you did! I can see the two of you now: "She's always been crazy about you, my boy. So why not pop along to Suffolk?"' she added, cruelly mimicking her grandfather's voice.

'That is *not* what happened,' Antonio retorted fiercely. 'Yes, I called to see Sir Robert. And, yes, I did discuss with him, man to man, the state of my current difficulties and also my future hopes for the family business in Spain.'

'Ah! So we're getting some of the truth—at last!'

'However, I can assure you, Gina, that the only time your name was mentioned was in relation to the fact that you were managing the Ipswich office where my shipment of wine was likely to be found.'

'Oh, really?' She gave a harsh, derisory hoot of laughter.

'I swear that what I say *is* the truth!' he thundered. 'In fact, I have only kept one piece of information from you. Which is that, during lunch that day, your grandfather told me that he had not long to live. But he did not want you to know, and so I respected his wishes. And that,' he added, spinning around on his heel to face her, 'that is the *only* piece of information which I have kept hidden from you.'

'Well, my grandfather is no longer here to prove or disprove what you've just said, is he?' she retorted angrily. 'And, in any case, the whole scenario which I've outlined to you fits together like a glove.'

'*Dios!*' he exploded, before swearing violently in Spanish under his breath. 'What do I have to do to get the truth into your stupid head?'

'Oh, it's all in my "stupid head", is it? Well, your uncle doesn't seem to think so. Nor does Carlotta! And since she informed me that she is working *so* closely with you at the moment—presumably both in and out of bed—I can only suppose that Carlotta knows what she's talking about!'

'If a husband and wife do not have any trust in one another *they have nothing*!' he told her fiercely. 'And yet you...you are willing to accept that evil woman's word over mine?'

'Damn right I am!' she lashed out. 'Because I reckon you two are just as bad as each other. So, don't you *ever* lay a hand on me again. Quite frankly,' she added scathingly, 'the thought of you touching me after having been with Carlotta makes me feel physically ill!'

He stood staring at her silently for some moments, his dark eyes blank and unfathomable.

'I ask myself why it is that you set such a very low premium on yourself, Gina?' he said finally, in a bitterly harsh, cruel voice, heavily laden with contempt.

'And it seems that you do not think very highly of me, either, *no*?'

'I…I think that you are…*despicable*!' she cried, her voice still echoing around the room when there came the sound of a sharp knock on the study door.

'The limousine is here to take you to the memorial service, madam,' Harold informed her, before taking one quick glance at their stiff, angry figures and quickly withdrawing from the room.

Whenever Gina recalled her grandfather's memorial service in later years, she was never able to repress a shudder at the memory of what was quite the worst, most desperately unhappy day of her entire life.

Compounding the perfectly normal deep sorrow she felt at the loss of her only relative was the ever-widening gulf which now clearly lay between herself and Antonio.

Forced to leave the house by the arrival of the limousine, she and her husband had no opportunity to talk privately, either in the vehicle itself or before and after the service.

To give Antonio his due, he stood dutifully and conscientiously by her side. But, while he might appear to be supportive, there was absolutely no comfort to be had from his tall, rigidly tense figure, or the austere, harshly forbidding expression on his face.

The journey home from the church was, if anything, even more unpleasant that the one they'd taken earlier that morning. Obviously her accusations and his angry, furious denial of any or all wrong doing, together with his own recriminations concerning her lack of trust in him, appeared to have erected a large barrier between them.

Quite where they went from here, she had no idea. After all, she told herself as they walked silently back into the house, after such a cataclysmic row what *could* they say to one another? And that was clearly a question which had also occurred to Antonio.

As soon as they had entered the house, she ran quickly upstairs to her bedroom, in search of some aspirins to soothe the deep, painful throbbing of the tension headache which had plagued her for most of the day.

But, having just decided to lie down on her bed for a while, in the hope of giving the medication a chance to begin working, it was only a few minutes later that she heard the door of the bedroom being thrown violently open.

'There seems no point in me staying in this house any longer. Especially as I am most clearly not welcome,' Antonio announced in a cold, hard voice.

'Moreover, I have much to occupy me in Jerez. Many problems which need to be addressed. Which is why I am intending to return to Spain tonight.'

Gingerly sitting up on the bed, and putting a shaky hand to her painful head, Gina muttered helplessly, 'But...but, we need to talk. I mean, we can't just...'

'Oh, no!' His furiously angry glinting black eyes flicked contemptuously over her trembling figure. 'I have no intention of listening to any more "talk" from you, Gina. In fact, with your having made plain your feelings about me, I cannot imagine we have anything to say to one another. Either now—or in the future!'

And then he was gone. Leaving only the noise of the door, slammed loudly in his wake, to echo around the bedroom, together with the sound of muffled sobs as Gina wept for both her broken heart and the loss of her husband.

In fact, how she managed to get through the next few days Gina had absolutely no idea. However, the imperative need to get a grip on the business empire left to her by her grandfather in many ways proved to be her salvation.

It was a desperately lonely life, of course. But at least there was little time to think about her own problems when there were so many questions and issues regarding the company to be dealt with.

Unfortunately, as she had always feared, having to take over the reins from someone who'd never been prepared to delegate an inch of his authority was proving to be incredibly difficult. And she had to—right from the start—put up with the fact that she and the general manager of the Pall Mall shop actively disliked each other.

However, she knew that she must ignore that fact—and the frequent, semi-snide remarks of the manager, just this side of outright rudeness. Because all her energies had to be directed into trying to bring some sort of order and method into the company.

All of which meant that she wasn't just rushed off her feet at work—she was also having to read her way through the files every night in a desperate effort to familiarise herself with the company's business.

Which at least had the merit of sending her to bed totally and utterly exhausted, with little or no time in which to weep over the cold embers of her very brief, disastrous marriage. Because, since returning to Spain after her grandfather's memorial service, she'd not heard another word from Antonio.

Well, I hope he's enjoying himself with that bitch

Carlotta! she told herself grimly, very late one night when she'd been unable to sleep, and had gone downstairs to the kitchen, to make herself a cup of tea.

But, despite almost wincing with pain at the thought of her husband and the sexy Spanish girl entwined together, she didn't really—in her heart of hearts—believe that Antonio had been two-timing her with Carlotta. They might have had an affair in the past, of course. But every ounce of feminine intuition Gina possessed was telling her that during his brief courtship and marriage to *her* he had not been sexually involved with any other woman.

On the other hand, her wild accusations—made in the heat and torment of their cataclysmic quarrel, and designed to hurt him as much as he'd wounded her—might well have driven him back into Carlotta's arms. But there was nothing she could do about that. And, after all, adultery was probably a slightly less important sin than falsely pretending to be in love with her in order to gain a large amount of money from her grandfather. The fact that she found the idea of Antonio and Carlotta together far more hurtful only went to prove that she was just a pathetically feeble woman.

However, as the weeks went by, and the new computers, together with upgraded phone and fax lines, were installed in all the offices of the company, Gina felt that she was at least managing to bring some fresh air and modern methods into an antiquated business. And, although she tried to convince herself that she loathed the rotten man who'd clearly married her under false pretences, Gina found herself feeling at least some sympathy for Antonio, who'd faced exactly the same problems when taking over his family company.

She was also aware, of course, that he must be very busy, since the future of his business would rise or fall on the results of the forthcoming grape harvest in Jerez.

Which was one reason, apart from her own stiff-necked pride, why she struggled to cope on her own with some very serious problems of supply and delivery. But when she discovered a massive embezzling of funds, by the general manager whom she'd always disliked and distrusted, Gina knew that she must act quickly to halt the rot. That, in fact, she had no one else to turn to but Antonio.

'Yes, of course I'm well aware that you've got your own problems,' she ground out through gritted teeth, when at last reaching Antonio by phone at his office in Spain.

'Believe me—I wouldn't *dream* of asking for your help if I could avoid doing so,' she added bitterly, flinching at the icy chill in his voice, which was positively arctic, before briefly explaining her problem.

'The fact is...' She hesitated, before taking a deep breath and admitting the truth. 'The fact is that I simply haven't enough experience to know what to do about the situation. My first instinct was to sack the guy outright, and press criminal charges. But I soon realised that it might be disastrous for the business. So, what do I do now? Just let him go quietly, and put up with the loss?'

'I'm too busy to consider the problem at the moment,' Antonio informed her. 'However, I will give it some thought and possibly come back to you later,' he added, before quickly terminating the call.

'Well, that was a complete bloody waste of time!' she ground out angrily, before slamming down the phone. She might have known that forcing herself to eat humble pie—and freely admitting that she didn't know the answer to a difficult problem—would be useless as far as Antonio was concerned.

Which was why she was totally astonished, on returning home the next day, to find her husband waiting for her in the study.

'What on earth are you doing here?' she gasped, quickly clutching hold of the back of a chair as she felt herself going unaccountably weak at the knees.

'I *am* still your husband—however much you may prefer to forget that fact,' he told her coldly.

'I'm sorry...I didn't mean to be rude. I was just surprised...that's all,' she heard herself explaining, feeling extraordinary light-headed.

Which wasn't surprising, she told herself some time later, as they sat in the formal dining room, both hardly touching their food. He had apparently already eaten a meal on the flight from Spain, while she...she was trying to deal with the extremely distressing, highly embarrassing fact that she was still wildly sexually attracted to her husband.

Dashing upstairs to the bedroom earlier, she'd been in a complete panic. Not only trying to think what to wear for dinner, but also attempting to come to terms with the fact that the mere sight of Antonio had set her heart pounding almost out of control. And she'd had no problem in recognising the feelings of sick excitement, and the tight clenching in the pit of her stomach, as hard evidence that she still wanted him—as much as ever.

Luckily—and mostly thanks to Harold, who'd smoothly given the impression that he and Gina were merely welcoming Antonio back from a routine business trip—they'd managed to get through the meal in a fairly civilised manner.

'You will have to let your manager go quietly and take the loss. Yes, I know it's maddening,' Antonio told her now, with a cold, wintry smile, as he picked at a piece of cheese and sipped his glass of red wine. 'But you must maintain the good name of the company—and make sure it never happens again.'

'Yes...yes, I suppose that makes sense,' she muttered, trying to concentrate on what he was saying. 'But I'm not quite sure how to go about it? Do I have to give him a reference? Or should I...?'

'I have arranged to stay over here for a few days to sort out this problem for you,' Antonio said, and once again the lofty, condescending note in his voice set her teeth on edge. 'It will clearly be necessary to appoint a new manager. And advice must be taken from your lawyer, as well as informing the bank of the situation.'

Tempting though it was to tell him to get lost, Gina knew that she was just going to have to bite the bullet. Even if the last thing she wanted was to have to deal with Antonio, she had no alternative. Not if she wanted to save her business.

Actually, she supposed she ought to be grateful that he hadn't heaped recriminations on her head, she told herself later that night, having quickly made her excuses and escaped upstairs to her bedroom after Harold had served them both after-dinner coffee.

In fact, she realised as she slipped into bed and turned out the light, Antonio had actually—if somewhat patronisingly—congratulated her on what she'd managed to achieve so far. Which was possibly why she'd proved to be so weak. So careful not to upset the apple cart, Gina had done her best to keep all conversation at dinner well away from the hugely irreconcilable, yawning gulf which lay so heavily between them.

Just as Gina closed her eyes and drifted into sleep the situation existing between herself and Antonio took a turn for which she was totally unprepared.

Having arranged for Antonio to sleep in one of the large guest rooms, she was startled to be awoken by the presence of his warm body slipping into her bed.

Her astonished cry was muffled as his mouth closed firmly over her lips, his hands sliding slowly and enticingly over her breasts and hips, the soft touch of his fingers gently calming her initial fear and trembling as his lips moved sensuously over hers, arousing a response she seemed helpless to either control or conceal.

As the treacherous warmth invaded her quivering body, there was nothing she could do to prevent the soft seduction of his lips and hands from arousing her starved emotions. Bemused as she was by the burning heat flooding her mind and body, she knew that Antonio was deliberately using his sexual expertise as a potent weapon. And it was one to which she was, alas, highly vulnerable.

'It seems that you *do* want me to touch you after all...' he breathed softly in her ear. 'Is that so? Do you want to feel my hands on your body?' he added, as she ardently responded in the darkness to the erotic touch of his fingers brushing over her swollen nipples.

'Well?' he demanded harshly. 'Do you want me?'

A deep, helpless shudder rippled through her body. 'Yes...yes, I want you,' she whispered, trapped in a dense mist of raging passion, and oblivious of anything other than the driving, desperate compulsion to surrender to his possession. Her desire and need of him was so intense that it was like a deep physical pain.

'*Bueno…!*' he growled. But she barely heard the husky note of triumph in his voice, her whole being absorbed by the scorching, searing touch of the hands and mouth now setting fire to her flesh.

Engrossed with her own emotional hunger, she wasn't sure if she imagined his low, deep groan as he impatiently parted her legs and finally entered her with a hard, driving thrust. Her own emotions responded to the pulsating rhythm of his powerful body with a frantic, erotic intensity that devoured them both, before the white-hot heat of their mutual lust and passion exploded in a shimmering starburst of light and power.

Afterwards, as they lay silently together in the dark, she forced herself to murmur, 'Why?'

'Because, Gina, you are still my wife. Because, contrary to what you believe, I am *not* the sort of man who commits adultery. And because…because it was plainly obvious to me, even over dinner, that you were consumed by a desperate need of my body,' he added, with a devastatingly cruel, low rumble of sardonic laughter, before quietly returning to his own room.

CHAPTER SEVEN

SHIVERING as she paid off the taxi, Gina moved swiftly across the wet pavement and up the steps to the front door of the large house in Pall Mall.

England on a hot summer's day was one thing. But on a dark, damp and dismal day in November it was quite another, she told herself glumly, fishing in her purse for her keys.

'You're late, madam,' Harold said reprovingly, hurrying across the hall as she entered the house, taking her briefcase and helping to remove her damp overcoat. 'Did you have a good meeting?'

'Yes, I think it went quite well,' she told him with a slight smile, before glancing swiftly down at her watch. If she didn't want to miss the beginning of the opera at Covent Garden tonight, she was going to have to get a move on.

'Shall I put your briefcase in the study?'

'Yes, please,' she said, adding as she paused with her foot on the first step of the staircase, 'Can you remind Anna that I'm entertaining some corporate clients and won't be needing dinner tonight?'

'Will Don Antonio be flying over from Spain to join you?' Harold asked casually, carefully not looking at her as she began mounting the stairs.

'No, I'm afraid that my husband can't make it this week. He's...er...he is far too busy at the moment,' she told him, despising herself for maintaining the charade of being one half of a happily married couple.

'Well, I hope you won't be too late, madam,' he said sternly over his shoulder as he walked towards the study. 'If you'll forgive me for saying so, you've been looking rather tired and drawn lately.'

Gina gave a snort of wry amusement. 'Thanks a bunch! You certainly know how to make a woman feel really terrific, Harold,' she called down over the banister. But his only reply was a low rumble of laughter as he continued his stately progress down the corridor.

She was going to have to do something about Harold and his wife Anna, Gina told herself as she continued slowly mounting the stairs to her bedroom. But what?

Having served her grandfather for many years—certainly as long as she could remember—both his man-servant and the cook-housekeeper had been generously provided for in his will. Which was why she'd been totally surprised to learn that instead of moving to the country, to enjoy their quiet and peaceful retirement, they'd both firmly insisted on remaining to look after her, here in London. Where she was, quite frankly, rattling around like a small pea in a large pod.

In fact, it was clearly time she decided what she was going to do about this enormous house. It seemed crazy to keep on living here, in solitary splendour, being looked after by two elderly, if devoted servants. Maybe she'd do better to find herself a large, glamorous apartment somewhere nearby? And thereby release Harold and Anna from what they clearly saw as their duty and responsibility to look after her.

But that, like so many other decisions in the pipeline, would undoubtedly have to wait its turn.

With a tired sigh she walked through into her dressing room, opening the cupboard doors and trying to think what to wear tonight.

Entertaining business clients in the wine trade wasn't something she'd ever had to do before. Although she had acted as hostess to her grandfather while she'd still been living here, before taking over the branch office in Suffolk.

However, after consultation with Margaret, her grandfather's secretary, who'd been kind enough to stay on and work with her, she'd eventually decided that her best option, where possible, was to take them to the opera.

'Your grandfather used to say that it saved him from having to spend long hours involved in boring conversation with equally boring people,' Margaret had told her with a grin.

'A good point!' Gina had laughed. And, since she loved going to the opera, those corporate clients who didn't would just have to lump it.

And besides, she consoled herself, selecting a pair of long black silk trousers and a simple scoop-necked sleeveless black silk top under a deep crimson evening cardigan in panne-velvet, the new Covent Garden Opera House needed the money provided by rich businessmen. Even if she deplored the fact that some of them had been known to spend most of the evening fast asleep!

Returning to the bedroom, she switched on the radio beside her bed, kicking off her shoes before slowly removing the gold earrings and necklace which she normally wore during the day.

While she wouldn't have confessed it to a living soul, she felt dreadfully lonely living all alone in this large house. The quiet background noise of various programmes and music on the radio helped to banish the oppressive silence.

Quite why the house should have felt quite different when her grandfather had been alive, she had no idea. Especially since he'd been virtually confined to his study. But since his sudden death she'd found herself becoming increasingly depressed and lonely.

So—what else is new? she asked herself wryly, walking through into the bathroom and turning on the shower. She knew only too well the reasons which lay behind her present life of utter desolation and deep unhappiness.

Even if she had hoped for some sort of partial reconciliation following Antonio's unexpected visit to London—and after the way he'd made love to her, she had no longer been sure *what* she wanted—Gina had been doomed to disappointment.

'I have decided that it is in the best interests of both your company and mine if the outside world assumes we are still a happily married couple,' he'd announced the next morning, preparing to accompany her to the office to sort out the problems arising from the theft by her manager.

'Outside confidence in a business is essential if a company is to thrive and be successful. And you cannot afford any gossip in the trade—nor allow anyone to assume that you are not in full control.'

'Are you saying that I can't run my own business?' she'd demanded angrily.

'No. I'm sure, given time, you will prove to be a competent businesswoman,' he'd told her in the same cold, patronising tone of voice which he'd used the night before. 'But at the moment you are highly vulnerable, with your employees depending on the firm hand of management at the head of the company.

'Which is why,' he'd continued, in the face of her silent, frustrated acknowledgement that he was quite right, 'I have decided that we will maintain the illusion, as far as the outside world is concerned, that we have a happy marriage. And why I will be paying regular visits to London, to deal with any problems which may have arisen in my absence.'

And that had been that, Gina now told herself glumly, sighing as she blow-dried her long, pale blonde hair. Unfortunately—and what had made the situation almost unbearable, as far as she was concerned—they were both well aware of just how much she needed him. Both in her business...and in her bed.

As it had turned out, that first visit by Antonio had set a pattern for the months that followed.

Other than during the grape harvest, he had flown over from Spain every few weeks, staying for just a day or two to help sort out any problems she might have with her family business.

Every night that he'd spent under the roof of the house in Pall Mall he had, at some point in the early hours of the morning, slipped quietly into her bed. And each and every time he had fiercely demanded that she acknowledge her need of him.

Goodness knows, she'd tried to steel herself against his fatal attraction. So many occasions she'd been utterly determined to lock her bedroom door and finally put an end to the façade. But...somehow...she'd never been able to force herself to do it.

Despite scornfully reviling herself for being such a pathetically feeble woman, she hadn't been capable of resisting her desperate, overwhelming need for the warmth and strength of his body. Quite shamelessly she'd eagerly welcomed his enticingly soft, erotic caress, ardently and wantonly giving herself to him in the darkness; their lovemaking had been conducted virtually in silence, and was never...ever...referred to in the light of day.

Gina hated and despised herself for being so weak, for desperately counting the days until his next visit...and the next. But it seemed that if she couldn't live with him neither was she able to live without him, despite the stark knowledge of how he had abused her love by seducing her into their travesty of a marriage.

Unfortunately, it seemed as though she wasn't as hard and tough as she'd like to think.

In fact, it had become increasingly obvious, lately, that she couldn't cope with the nervous strain of the emotional roller-coaster on which she seemed to be trapped. And when, after a long board meeting, she'd returned to her office only to find herself inexplicably bursting into tears, Gina had known that she was no longer capable of existing within the farce of her marriage.

A fact which she'd somehow eventually managed to force herself to tell Antonio the last time she'd seen her husband, a few weeks ago.

'We can't keep on like this,' she'd finally managed to summon the courage to tell him one evening, when she'd returned late from the office to find him sitting in her grandfather's study.

'I don't know what the answer is—maybe a divorce?' she'd added with a heavy sigh. 'All I know is...our present way of life is tearing me apart. I'm simply not able to hack it anymore. And I don't suppose that you're gaining any pleasure from it, either.'

'No. I am not,' he'd agreed in the cold, hard voice which he'd used when speaking to her ever since their major quarrel all those months ago.

'Well...it doesn't look as if there's anything more to say, does there?' she'd said. And, since he'd made no further comment, firmly changing the subject to talk about a recent business problem, she'd eventually given a weary shrug, before turning to leave the room and walking slowly upstairs to her bedroom.

When he had not slipped into bed beside her that night, she'd realised that he, too, recognised that their miserably unhappy marriage of convenience was now virtually at an end.

If only one could just turn off the tap of love as easily as one could apparently terminate a marriage, she thought dismally, going back into the bedroom and quickly slipping into the clothes which she'd laid out on the bed.

The truth of which she'd been sharply reminded of only last week, when a thick envelope had arrived from Roxana.

It had contained a brief letter from her old friend, who was now, of course, also her sister-in-law, giving news of her forthcoming marriage to a fellow actor. It seemed that he was, to Roxana's amusement, regarded by her family as highly suitable, being a younger son of a large aristocratic family.

Pleased to hear the happy news of her old friend, Gina had been touched to see that Roxana had also included an official invitation to her wedding—due to be held at Bourgos, in the North of Spain, in a few weeks' time.

Not that she could possibly accept the invitation, Gina had told herself quickly. While she and her old friend had, of course, remained in touch—although they were always careful to avoid any mention of Antonio—her attendance at this sort of family gathering would not be welcome. Especially if, as seemed highly likely, she and her husband were about to divorce one another.

However, just as she'd been about to throw the envelope on the fire, she'd seen that Roxana had also enclosed a cutting which she'd clearly torn from a Spanish magazine detailing the news, views and social chit-chat of Spanish high society.

And there, in the middle of the page—under which Roxana had scribbled in thick black ink: *'What are you going to do about this?'*—had been a photograph of Antonio.

Pictured at some prestigious wine festival, he was smiling broadly at the camera. But he was not alone. Because there, clinging tightly to his arm, was the oh-so-voluptuous figure of Carlotta Perez, the smouldering gleam in her large black eyes practically setting fire to the page as she pressed herself closely to the tall figure of her handsome escort.

Almost gasping with pain, Gina had sat huddled in the large leather chair for a long time, before wearily throwing the cutting into the fire.

And now, Gina told herself, as she picked up her evening purse and prepared to leave for the opera, if she'd learned nothing else during these deeply unhappy months, she'd been brought face to face with one inescapable, harsh fact of life.

Whatever the outcome of her marriage, there was going to be no early release from the deep, emotional feelings which she clearly still had for her husband.

*   *   *

The wonderfully Baroque dining room of the Ritz Hotel was buzzing with noise as Gina was led to the table where her godmother was sitting.

'I'm sorry to be so late,' Gina murmured, giving the older woman a quick kiss on the cheek before sitting down and picking up the menu.

'Hmm...and you had *so* far to come today, too!' Joyce Frazer teased.

'Ha!' Gina grinned, conceding the point, since both her home and office were only just down the road, while her godmother had come all the way down from Suffolk to spend the day shopping in London. 'No, it was pressure of business, I'm afraid,' she admitted.

'Really, darling! You're looking far too thin,' the older woman said with concern, when they'd placed their order. 'It doesn't suit you,' she added firmly, her eyes flicking over the lines of strain and the deep shadows beneath Gina's normally sparkling blue eyes as she picked at the food in front of her. 'What's wrong?'

However, when the girl merely gave a slight shrug of her slim shoulders, Joyce Frazer decided to take the matter into her own hands.

'Am I correct in assuming that this very strange semi-detached marriage of yours is not going too well?'

'Well...er...I think that's probably a fair description of the situation,' Gina admitted slowly.

'Which is hardly surprising,' the older woman drawled. 'In my experience, a relationship between a man and a woman is difficult enough even when they're living permanently under the same roof. But since your husband appears to reside mainly in Spain,' she added, 'I imagine that must present some difficulties.'

'Yes. It…it's not easy.'

When the girl didn't say any more, merely continuing to push the food around her plate, Joyce said, 'It's no good sitting there wreathed in gloom and generally looking like a wet weekend. If your marriage is in trouble, I think you'd better tell me about it. And then we'll have to see what we can do to try and solve the problem.

'Come on, Gina,' she added impatiently. 'You of all people ought to know that I'm *not* going to let you off the hook. Not until I've got the whole story out of you. From start to finish!'

Gina gave a muffled snort of laughter. Her darling godmother was, as usual, quite right. It was hopeless to try and keep anything from the older woman. She'd always seemed to know when something was wrong in Gina's life, and had, more often than not, been able to give her extremely good advice.

And so, haltingly at first, Gina explained the basically insoluble problem which lay at the heart of her marriage to Antonio.

'So, while the sex was and is great—everything else is dust and ashes?' Joyce murmured, horrified to learn that her beloved goddaughter had been carrying such an unhappy, heavy burden for so many months. 'Well…I'm very sorry to hear that your Antonio should have turned out to have such feet of clay.' She frowned. 'But I must say that it doesn't seem to quite add up.'

'What do you mean?'

Joyce Frazer gave a sigh and shrugged her slim, elegant shoulders. 'Well, let's face it, darling—he *is* fairly wealthy in his own right, as well as being quite extraordinarily handsome. So if he'd been solely concerned with obtaining money to prop up his family's wine-making business, I can assure you that there are hundreds of women on the continent—and in Spain itself, of course—who are *far* richer than you are ever going to be. *And* many of them have a family tree as long as your arm.'

'So?' Gina muttered dully.

'So…if gorgeous, handsome and independently wealthy Don Antonio Ramirez could have easily found himself a rich and very well-connected wife in Spain—why didn't he just get on with it?'

'I…I don't understand.'

Joyce sighed. 'Darling—don't be so dim! If Antonio wanted a rich wife in a hurry, why go to all the trouble of travelling to Britain? And besides…is it *really* beyond the bounds of possibility that Antonio could have fallen violently in love with you the first moment he set eyes on you?

'Believe me, it does happen,' she added, as Gina gave a snort of derisive laughter.

'Sorry.' Gina shrugged. 'That's a nice idea, of course. But I don't think it's got any relevance to what happened to me,' she muttered, staring blindly down at the plate in front of her.

'Well, now you've outlined your problem to me, darling, I suppose I'd better try and come up with a solution.'

'If only it were that easy,' her goddaughter told her with a tired smile.

'Well…what we have here,' Joyce told her reflectively, 'would seem to be a case of a *very* strong physical attraction between two people who, in every other respect, appear to be completely at odds with one another. Am I correct so far?'

Gina nodded. 'Unfortunately, yes—you're absolutely right.'

'Which leads me to the inescapable conclusion that in order to resolve matters—and sort out the deep problems between you—it will be necessary to find an opportunity for you and your clearly prickly, difficult husband to sit down and talk things through.'

'Yes, well…that might have been the sensible answer to the problem a month or two ago. But I'm afraid matters have gone rapidly downhill lately.'

There was a long silence as her godmother carefully considered everything Gina had said. Then she said, 'I think there is a possibility that you still might be able to save your marriage. It all comes down to one or two very important questions.'

'And they are…?'

'Firstly—do you still love Antonio? And I think,' she said with a smile, 'that you've made it abundantly clear that you do. And the next question has to be: what are you going to do about it?'

Gina gazed at her in astonishment. 'Are you actually suggesting that I…I should just forget what he did to me?'

'No, of course not. But I *am* suggesting that you take a good, hard look at the situation. You appear to truly love this man. And it's obvious that he also feels very deeply for you. Which isn't hard to work out, since he doesn't seem to be able to keep his hands off you!' she added, giving a light ripple of laughter at the tide of bright crimson flooding over her goddaughter's face.

'So, is it merely pride which is preventing you and Antonio from sorting out your problems? From sitting down and having a long, sensible talk to one another?

Because, if so, then clearly one of you will have to take the first step. And—I have to be honest—I don't think your proud Spanish husband could ever bring himself to do it. So it looks as if it will have to be you, doesn't it?'

'Oh, no...no, I couldn't possibly...'

'Take my word for it,' Joyce told her firmly. 'Pride is a wretched, icy cold bedfellow. It's the root cause of most divorces—where nice, ordinary people can become so embittered and hostile simply because either they can't admit that they might have been at fault or bring themselves to forgive those who have sinned in some way. Believe me, darling,' she added sternly, 'there is absolutely *no* room for pride in a marriage!

'But one of you *has* to take the initiative,' Joyce continued. 'And since I think we can agree that it will have to be you, Gina, there's only one answer: you're simply going to have to seduce your husband. Both back into your bed and permanently back into your life.'

Gina gave an unhappy huff of laughter. 'You don't seem to understand. We're not talking of a simple case of adultery which I can either forgive or not, as I see fit. And this *isn't* just a case of pride. What I'm facing is a fundamentally *moral* question. Did Antonio use underhand methods to get me to marry him for the sake of my grandfather's money? And I must say that I believe he did. And *that* is something that I find indefensible. And no amount of sensible discussion is going to make it any better!'

'No, darling—of course it's not!' Joyce Frazer agreed. 'But you were telling me earlier about the invitation you'd just received to Roxana's wedding. I don't know Bourgos, of course. Or Roxana's arrangements. But it shouldn't be beyond the wit of a determined woman to find *some* way in which to remind her husband *exactly* why he married his wife in the first place…'

Satisfied to note that her last remark had clearly hit home, and that she'd at least given the younger woman something to think about, Joyce adroitly changed the subject by enquiring as to how Gina was coping with her new responsibilities in the wake of her grandfather's death.

It was only when the younger girl was preparing to take her leave that her godmother gave her a warm hug, whispering in her ear, 'Go to Spain and seduce him, darling. Believe me, the mixture of deep, true love and strong sexual attraction is a *very* powerful weapon!'

It was all very well for her godmother to suggest that her problems could be easily resolved by merely seducing her husband. But, as she'd told Joyce, that simply wasn't an option she was prepared to consider. Her marriage to Antonio was obviously coming to its close, the gulf between them being simply too wide to be bridged.

In fact, the more she thought about it during the next few days, the more Gina realised that any idea of attending Roxana's wedding was simply not acceptable.

For one thing she would have to meet all the Ramirez family relations, and that could prove to be extremely embarrassing for them all. Even if Antonio *had* managed not to talk about his disintegrating marriage, surely some of the family must have a very good idea that all was not well between himself and Gina?

And then there was the question of Antonio himself.

He would almost certainly *not* be pleased to see her. And there seemed no point in putting her own still-fragile emotions through such a maelstrom.

Which was why she'd made up her mind to politely but firmly refuse the wedding invitation when she received a telephone call from the bride herself.

'But *of course* you must come to my wedding!' Roxana cried. 'It won't be the same without you, Gina. Not at all.'

'Look, it's not that I don't want to come,' Gina explained. 'But when I had a look at the map of Spain, it seemed as though Bourgos was absolutely miles from anywhere. Certainly quite a long haul from the nearest airport, which appears to be Bilbao. So, I'm afraid that...'

'No! I'm not going to allow you to try to wriggle out of this,' Roxana told her firmly, before adding with a slight laugh, 'I know you too well—you're just suffering from cold feet about this situation. Yes?'

I couldn't have put it better myself, Gina thought, desperately trying to think of some other valid excuse for avoiding the confrontation which lay ahead.

'Really, you have no need to worry. For one thing, I will not tell my brother that you are coming to my wedding,' Roxana continued, clearly determined not to let her old friend off the hook. 'Besides, we are sisters now. *Sí*? So you can trust me in this.'

Gina gave a heavy sigh. 'But if you don't tell Antonio that I'm coming it's more than likely that he'll be *very* angry. Especially if the first he knows about it is when he sees me there, in the church. In fact, he's going to go bananas—and well you know it, Roxana!'

'Ah, Gina...'

'And...and besides—where would I stay?'

'Oh, *please*...I must have my oldest friend at my wedding,' Roxana wailed. *'I must!'*

'Well, you know that I really don't want to let you down, but...'

'You can leave everything to me,' her old schoolfriend said quickly, clearly sensing that Gina was weakening. 'I will make all the arrangements. There will be a limousine to meet you at Bilbao Airport, and I will book you into the largest and most exclusive hotel.'

'That sounds very grand!'

'It is,' Roxana assured her, explaining that the hotel lay just outside Bourgos, on the road to Madrid. It was also a member of the prestigious *Relais et Châteaux* group, so Gina could be assured of luxurious surroundings. And if there should be any problems, at least she'd be miserable in comfort.

'Thanks a bunch!'

'Believe me, I have your best interests at heart,' her friend told her, adding in a more serious voice, 'I ask you to trust me, Gina. And, you know, it really is *very* important to me that I have my oldest and dearest friend at my wedding. So, please come. Yes?'

How could she resist such a plea? Gina asked herself with a heavy sigh.

And so, despite knowing that she was going to live to severely regret her decision, she reluctantly agreed, not only to attend the wedding, but also to gratefully accept the arrangements Roxana was making on her behalf.

CHAPTER EIGHT

IT HADN'T been exactly the easiest of journeys, Gina told herself, waiting patiently with the other passengers for the luggage carousel to begin revolving in front of her at Bilbao Airport.

It was far too late for regrets now, of course. But why she'd allowed her arm to be twisted by Roxana and be persuaded to attend her old school friend's wedding, she had absolutely no idea. Quite frankly, Gina thought nervously, she was becoming more and more certain that in accepting the invitation she was making a very grave and serious mistake.

Quite apart from anything else, the weeks before Christmas were the busiest time of year in the wine trade. As a main importer of fine wines, sherries and liquors, her firm was in the midst of taking last-minute orders and delivering urgently needed supplies to wine merchants and supermarkets throughout the United Kingdom. And she needed to spend time away from her desk like she needed a hole in the head!

Which was why she'd left her packing to the last minute, still throwing things into her suitcase early this morning, before leaving for the airport.

'Hurry up, madam—the chauffeur is waiting for you,' Harold had called out, carrying her suitcase out to the car as she'd hurried down the stairs, giving his wife, Anna, a quick kiss and grabbing that morning's post from the hall table before tumbling into the back of the large black limousine.

Sinking back on the soft leather seat as the vehicle had drawn smoothly out into the traffic around St James's Palace, Gina had been forced to admit that, once again, her husband was quite correct.

'This way you have of travelling around London in taxis is plainly ridiculous,' he'd informed her firmly on his last visit. 'Half the time you can't get hold of one—especially when it's raining—and for the last three days Margaret has confirmed that you've been late for important appointments simply because you had to wait for a taxi.'

'Leave Margaret alone!' Gina had snapped, fed up to the back teeth with the way practically everyone in the company, regarded Antonio with starry-eyed awe and reverence. The way they kowtowed to him anyone would think *he* owned Brandon's, she'd told herself grimly.

'You've charmed the socks off most of my employees. But Margaret is *my* secretary, and she reports only to *me*,' Gina had added, despite knowing that she was being extremely childish.

But for once Antonio hadn't given her one of his cold, chilly set-downs. In fact, he'd merely grinned with amusement before informing her that he had already arranged for the company to lease a large limousine for her, and engaged a chauffeur to drive it.

'Oh, great!' she'd ground out tersely. 'Another employee on the payroll. Just what I need when I'm trying to keep costs down!'

But over the past few weeks the chauffeur, Marvin, had almost become one of the family. Harold was, of course, still reserving judgement—mostly because, like Gina, he considered that he should have been consulted about the appointment. But since his wife,

Anna, was already feeding Marvin delicious tidbits in the kitchen, it was clearly only a matter of time before Harold and he became the best of friends.

It was, without doubt, a great boon to know that whenever she wanted to go anywhere—morning, noon or night—Gina never had to worry about transport. And it was clearly just her bad luck that Antonio— God rot him—had been proved right, yet again.

Jerked out of her reverie by a loud, clattering sound, Gina saw that the luggage carousel was beginning to revolve, with various pieces of passengers' luggage appearing on the conveyor belt. After collecting her suitcase, she was greatly relieved to find that Roxana's arrangements appeared to be working smoothly, as she was greeted by a uniformed chauffeur in the main concourse of the busy airport.

As the long black limousine left Bilbao's Sondika Airport, Gina settled back against the luxurious leather upholstery, beginning to feel slightly more reassured about the ordeal which lay in front of her.

Everything could still go pear-shaped, of course. And with her luck, undoubtedly would do so. But so far—so good. And, since the driver clearly had no English—and her Spanish was still woefully inadequate to carry on more than the very simplest of conversations—she settled back against the seat, closing her eyes and letting her mind drift over the likely problems which lay ahead.

It was a long journey, and Gina realised that she must have fallen asleep when she found herself being woken by the chauffeur's discreet cough as he drew up outside what appeared to be a very large mediaeval castle.

By the time she had checked in and was being

shown to her extraordinarily luxurious room, Gina was actually beginning to relax.

After tipping the porter who'd carried her luggage up to the room, Gina walked over to the elegant writing desk by the window and picked up the phone to call Roxana.

'So—you've arrived!' the bride-to-be sang out happily.

'Yes, I'm here. And I must thank you so much for the wonderfully smooth arrangements you've made for me so far. Incidentally—' she laughed '—this is an utterly *amazing* hotel! Absolutely wall-to-wall grandeur.'

'I thought you'd like it!'

'And how are all your arrangements going? You sound remarkably calm and serene for someone who's getting married tomorrow.'

'*No problema!*' Roxana told her, sounding totally relaxed and free of any worries. 'As it happens, I have a wonderfully efficient mother-in-law, whom I love dearly and who has insisted on taking care of all the really boring but essential details concerned with a wedding. So, lucky old me! All I have to do is to get dressed tomorrow and walk down the aisle with my dear brother Antonio. Simple, *no*?'

'Talking about your dear brother Antonio...' Gina hesitated for a moment. 'Where...er...where exactly is he staying? With you and your in-laws?'

'No. Unfortunately this house, while large, has not so many bedrooms. And it was felt that Isabella, Jaime and their children would be more comfortable here, rather than in a hotel. So...I'm not really exactly sure where Antonio is staying tonight. However,' Roxana added casually, 'I can, of course, find out for you, if you like?'

'No, thank you,' Gina said quickly. 'I'm feeling rather tired after the journey. And we will, of course, be seeing each other tomorrow, at your wedding,' she added, before wishing her old friend the best of luck and much happiness and putting down the phone.

If there was one thing about which she was quite certain, Gina told herself firmly, it was that she *really* didn't want to see Antonio tonight.

Principally, of course, because she had a good idea that he wasn't going to be at all pleased about her arrival in Spain. And that was putting it mildly! Antonio was going to be extremely annoyed at being kept in the dark. So when they did eventually come face-to-face, Gina was going to feel a good deal happier if the meeting took place amidst a large collection of guests at the wedding.

Deciding that she really couldn't face dining downstairs in the glamorous restaurant all on her own, Gina ordered a light meal from Room Service before deciding to have a long, hot bath.

But first she must unpack her luggage, and hang up in the wardrobe the outfit which she was intending to wear at tomorrow's wedding.

Having done so, it was only when she was putting her suitcase into a cupboard that she remembered her post—which she'd quickly grabbed that morning in her rush to the airport. She had quickly stuffed it into the wide outside pocket of her suitcase and promptly forgotten all about it. Until now.

'It's bound to be mostly bills,' she muttered out loud, quickly sorting through the envelopes to see if there was anything which looked at all urgent. But there was only one—from her lawyer—which Gina felt she probably ought to open.

Having read the letter through once, Gina sank down on to the bed, her head in a whirl as she gazed into space for some moments before forcing herself to read it again.

'I must apologise for the delay in writing to you,' her lawyer had begun, before explaining that he had recently been in hospital for a minor operation.

'However, having received a letter from your husband's Spanish lawyers (copy enclosed) I will require your instructions before proceeding with this matter...'

Briefly glancing at the photocopy of a letter, written in Spanish, from a firm of *notarios* in Cadiz, Gina returned to read carefully through what her own lawyer had said.

Boiled down to the bare essentials, it seemed that Antonio's Spanish lawyers had sent her lawyer a very stiff, curt letter, saying that their client had instructed them to return the money left to him by Sir Robert Brandon.

Not only had Don Antonio Ramirez been astonished to learn of the legacy following Sir Robert's death, but he had no wish or need to accept it. Moreover, his grandfather-in-law's request—that the sum involved should be used towards the modernisation of the Bodega Ramirez—was entirely unnecessary.

The funds to do so had already been arranged with a bank in Spain before Señor Don Antonio had left Spain for England and his first meeting with Sir Robert Brandon in London, earlier in the year. The signed contract between the Banco de Andalusia and the Bodega Ramirez was, of course, available for inspection by Señora Doña Georgina Ramirez, should she wish to satisfy herself as to its validity.

The Spanish lawyers were, therefore, returning the cheque forthwith—together with Señor Don Antonio Ramirez's firm insistence that he wished to hear no more on the subject.

'Oh, no...!' Gina gasped, as the full implications of the letter broke through the dazed confusion in her mind.

Oh, God! What on earth was she going to do now? Antonio *had* been telling her the truth—all the time. He had already raised the money he needed for his business *before* he'd set foot in England, and before that meeting with her grandfather. What was more— he had a signed document to prove it!

With her thoughts whirling and spinning out of control, Gina threw herself back on the bed, staring blindly up at the ceiling as she tried to come to terms with the fact that she...and *she* alone...was responsible for the total collapse and destruction of her happy marriage. That every single bit of heartache and lone- liness...all these months of desperate unhappi- ness...were the result of her own utterly foolish inabil- ity to believe the man whom she'd always—as long as she could remember—loved with all her heart.

How *could* she have been so stupid? *Why* hadn't she trusted him? Was she really so insecure that she'd let an elderly, confused man and a nasty, viciously spiteful woman sow such seeds of bitterness and dev- astation?

Totally stunned at the extent of her own folly, Gina slowly sat up on the bed, before stumbling like a sleep- walker into the bathroom.

Lying in the hot water, trying to come to terms with

the full, disastrous extent of what she'd done, it was only the fragrant and soothing bath oil which proved to be of any comfort. She was beyond tears. Dry-eyed, and staring blindly into the thick cloud of steam rising over the bath, she finally realised that, having been granted a brief glimpse of heaven, she was now trapped in a hell of her own making.

And there was nothing—*absolutely nothing*—she could do about it.

And when, some time later, she heard the door of her suite open, as she'd just finished towelling herself dry, Gina realised that the very last thing she wanted was the food she'd so carelessly ordered on her arrival.

However, she had no choice but to go through the motions of signing for the damn thing, she told herself grimly. Slipping on a light dressing gown and belting it up around her slim waist, she called out, 'I'm just coming,' before walking through into the main room of the suite.

Only to find herself coming to a sudden halt, quickly grabbing hold of the back of a nearby chair to stop herself from collapsing with shock.

Her sapphire-blue eyes growing wide with disbelief, she stared in horror at the tall, dark figure of a man clothed in an elegant black cashmere overcoat. While he, for his part, having clearly spun around at the sound of her voice, was staring at her with an expression of utter shock and incredulity.

'Gina!' Antonio exclaimed, his deep voice sounding hard and cold. 'What in the hell are *you* doing here?'

With her mind in a complete daze, she couldn't seem to be able to get a firm grip on the situation for some moments. And then the full horror of the problems which lay ahead began flooding into her mind.

Quite apart from anything else, it was clearly the worst possible time for a meeting with her husband— let alone after she'd just discovered that he was innocent of all her wild accusations.

Besides, it looked as if her previous fears, that he would be less than pleased to see her at the wedding, were absolutely spot-on. From the way his dark, angry eyes were glaring at her, it looked as if hell would freeze over before he'd be prepared to even give her the time of day.

'Is this some bad joke?' Antonio's dark eyebrows were drawn together in a deep frown. 'I demand to know what you're doing here,' he grated angrily.

'What am *I* doing here?' Gina gave a high-pitched, shrill burst of laughter. 'That is precisely the question I was going to ask *you*!'

'Don't be ridiculous,' he retorted curtly. 'This is my room, and…'

'Correction!' she snapped. 'This is *my* suite. There's probably been some error on the part of the hotel. I had no idea that you were staying here,' she added, wrapping her arms quickly about her trembling body. 'But I think you'll find it is merely a simple mistake, and…and that you've been shown to the wrong room.'

'*Absolutamente, no,*' he informed her firmly. 'Since I didn't make the booking, I checked the number on my arrival downstairs at Reception. And, as you can see…' he held up a key with the same room number as hers dangling from its shaft '…this is most definitely *my* room.'

'No, it's not!' Gina protested. 'I've got exactly the same key.'

She marched over to the small, elegant table beside

the main door of the suite of rooms, lifting up her key and walking back to show it to him.

'And besides,' she added firmly, 'Roxana made all the arrangements for my arrival. Since everything else seems to have gone like clockwork, it's obvious that you...'

'*Roxana?*' he exclaimed loudly, quickly seizing the key from her hand. Swiftly comparing the two matching numbers, he spun around on his heels, marching across the floor to pick up the telephone.

Following a rapid exchange in Spanish, far too fast for her to follow, he eventually slammed down the receiver, swearing violently under his breath.

'So it isn't your room after all?' she queried.

'On the contrary, my dear Gina, it is my room— and yours!' He gave a low rumble of harsh, sardonic laughter at the expression of consternation on her face. 'Yes, I'm afraid that we have both been booked into this room—under the names of Señor and Señora Ramirez. In fact, it seems that my dear sister Roxana has been very busy, does it not?'

Gina stared at him in openmouthed dismay. 'I...I don't believe it. Surely Roxana wouldn't have...? She couldn't...?'

'Unfortunately, it is now abundantly clear that she could—and she did. And believe me,' he added grimly, 'I intend to have a few hard words with the blushing bride!

'However, it is merely a small problem,' he continued, in a hard voice. 'It will be a simple matter for the hotel to find me another room.'

Trembling, and prey to conflicting emotions, Gina realised that although she'd been deeply apprehensive about this first meeting with Antonio, at least it was over and done with. He now knew she was in Spain, and would be attending the marriage tomorrow. So that was one hurdle out of the way.

Although how she was going to deal with the devastating information she'd just received, she had no idea. And this was hardly the time—or the place—to try and say she was sorry. Indeed, she had so *very* much to apologise for she hadn't even a clue where to start.

Immersed in her thoughts, Gina had only barely noticed Antonio picking up the phone to talk, once again, to the reception desk. And was therefore surprised when, for the second time in a few minutes, he slammed down the phone before slowly turning around to stare at her, a harsh and forbidding expression on his handsome, tanned face.

'It seems that my dear sister has been even cleverer than she imagined,' he said at last in icy tones. 'Because I have been informed that this hotel is booked solid—mostly, I regret to say, with guests attending my sister's wedding. They have no other room for you other than a small maid's room on the top floor.'

Gina stared at him for a moment, before giving a strangled snort of incredulous laughter.

'You *must* be joking!'

'No, of course I am not,' he snapped.

'But…but you can't *seriously* think that I…I'm going to go and spend the night in "a small maid's room on the top floor"!' she exclaimed. 'Besides…I was here first. And here I'm staying!' she announced, lifting her chin aggressively towards him.

'Don't be ridiculous!' he ground out, shrugging off his dark overcoat and throwing it, in what she could only think of as a highly possessive action, onto the large double bed.

'You cannot possibly expect *me* to sleep in a small, inferior room,' Antonio told her, sounding amazed that she should even be prepared to think the unthinkable. 'I am simply not prepared to discuss the matter.'

'*Oh, great!* You mean it's good enough for me, your poor old wife, but not for the grand Señor Don Antonio Ramirez?' she stormed, before it suddenly occurred to her that he just might…he just *could* be expecting that *awful* woman Carlotta Perez to be joining him.

Well! She certainly wasn't going to put up with *that*! Whether he liked it or not she was still his wife. And if he thought that he could just install his…his current mistress in this suite—he'd *definitely* got another think coming!

'If you think that I'm moving out of here to make way for your girlfriend…you're badly mistaken!' she ground out, almost beside herself with fury.

'*Que?*' He looked up from his briefcase, which he'd just placed on the small desk by the telephone. 'I don't know what you're talking about? What girlfriend?' he demanded angrily.

'Hah! I know all about you and that woman. I've seen the picture of the two of you in that Spanish magazine. And it was clear that she'd got *you* well and truly nailed to her mast!'

Antonio stared fixedly at her for a moment, before giving a slight shrug. 'You have said that you no longer want me, Gina. So why should you care about Carlotta?' he drawled coolly, the slight glimmer of sardonic amusement in his dark eyes adding fuel to the flames of her anger.

'As it happens, I couldn't care less!' Gina retorted, quickly trying to retrieve the situation. The last thing...the *very* last thing she wanted was to have Antonio suspecting that she might be jealous of the glamorous Spanish woman.

'However,' she continued, 'I just wanted to make it plain that *if* you've set up a sordid rendezvous here with her—or any other woman, for that matter— you're way out of luck. Because I'm *not* moving!'

'Oh, really?' He gave a harsh laugh. 'I think you'll find that the porter will be here in a moment or two, to escort both you and your luggage out of this suite!'

'Oh, really?' she echoed furiously, dearly wishing that she wasn't standing here in her bare feet. Because just at this moment she'd give everything she possessed for a pair of high-heeled pointed stiletto shoes—with which to give him a sharp kick in the shins!

'Well, have I got news for you!' she told him grimly. 'I have absolutely *no* intention of taking one step outside this bedroom suite.'

'Now, Gina...'

'What's more, I'm going back into the bathroom, and...and I may not be out for some hours!' she added, trembling with rage as she strode determinedly back into the adjoining bathroom, slamming the door loudly behind her before firmly turning the key in the lock.

This was all very well, Gina told herself, gradually simmering down as she paced up and down the large, luxurious bathroom. But she couldn't stay here for ever, could she?

So what the hell was she going to do? was the over-

riding question in her mind as she sank dispiritedly
down on to the small stool beside the bath.

Oh, Lord! First she'd made a complete pig's breakfast of her once happy marriage, and now she was
locked in a bathroom, with her very angry, thoroughly
irate husband on the other side of the door. If the situation hadn't been so damned tragic it would have
been totally hilarious!

Quickly reviewing the alternatives open to her—and
there seemed very few, if any—Gina realised that *any*
idea she might have had of attempting to apologise for
her part in the destruction of their marriage had just
flown out of the window.

Even thinking of trying to have some sort of reconciliation with that hard, angry man next door was
totally inconceivable.

While he might be cross with his sister, for so clum-
sily trying to bring him and his wife closer together,
he certainly wasn't happy about the situation in which
he now found himself. In fact, he was downright furious. Which wasn't surprising, she acknowledged
with a slight grimace. No one, least of all her proud
and imperious husband, liked to think that they'd been
manipulated by outside forces. And she wasn't at all
happy about the situation either.

Damn Roxana! Why couldn't the girl have just left
matters alone?

'Come out of there immediately!' Antonio called
out, banging imperiously on the door.

'No, I won't. Go away!' she retorted loudly, still
trying to think of a way to extricate herself from this
embarrassing situation.

She would, of course, have to leave this bathroom

fairly soon. But she was damned if she was going to do so just because her husband was shouting at her.

'Stop being so silly, Gina,' he said in a slightly quieter tone of voice. 'It's been a long day. And I need to wash and shave before having dinner.'

'That's just too bad!' she snapped from the other side of the door, finding some balm for her exhausted emotional state as she heard him muttering oaths in Spanish under his breath.

However, about ten minutes later, she was alerted by a soft tap on the door.

'It is patently ridiculous for the two of us to be behaving like children in this way,' she heard him say quietly. 'It is also clear that we have no choice but to share this room tonight. I have already phoned down to the restaurant, asking them to serve dinner for two up here in the suite. So…may I suggest that we both take a deep breath and come to our senses?'

There was a long pause before he added in softer tones, 'Come, *querida*—it is foolish for us to be so angry with each other, *no*?'

Well…he did seem to be offering an olive branch, Gina told herself. So she might as well be sensible and grab hold of it, while the going was good.

'All right,' she sighed, undoing the lock and slowly opening the door.

'I'm sorry that I seem to have been behaving childishly,' she admitted as she entered the room. 'It was a long flight from London, and…and I'm probably tired,' she added with a slight shrug of her slim shoulders.

'It has been a long day for me, too,' he admitted, brushing a weary hand through his thick black curly hair.

'I flew into Madrid from California yesterday. And I had so many meetings today that I only just caught the plane up here by the skin of my teeth. So, we are both tired, yes? Which is all the more reason,' he added, as she gave him a slow nod, 'for us, as you say in England, "to bury the hatchet" and try to have a pleasant dinner together, hmm?'

'That seems a sensible decision,' she agreed slowly, noting for the first time the deep lines of strain on his face. 'Why don't you have a bath? After all, dinner can wait, can't it?'

While Antonio was taking her good advice, and having a long soak in the bathtub, Gina took the opportunity of asking Room Service to send up a bottle of chilled champagne, as well as putting the delivery of their dinner back by an hour. And Room Service, in this wonderful hotel, seemed only too pleased to accept her new instructions.

God bless Roxana! At least she hadn't booked them both into some grotty hotel, which would have clearly made life a lot harder, more difficult than it already was at the moment. Although, bride or not, Antonio wasn't the only one who was looking forward to having a few hard words with her old schoolfriend.

As soon as the champagne was delivered, and the servant had left the room, she took the opportunity to quickly change into a long sapphire-blue velvet housecoat, which for some reason she'd thrown into her suitcase at the last moment.

What with one thing and another, she told herself, as she fastened a large string of pearls about her neck and matching pearl studs in her ears, it was going to be a tough evening. So...looking as smart as possible and putting on some make-up was the only defence in her armoury. Though Antonio seemed prepared to be civil, that was clearly the most she could expect.

She had no illusions that he would draw any false conclusions from that bottle of champagne, either, she told herself glumly. But she needed something to cheer herself up in this dire situation. And at least she could pretend for a few moments, while sipping the golden liquid, that her whole life and her marriage hadn't gone right down the tubes.

Actually, the champagne seemed to have been a rather good idea, Gina told herself some time later as she and Antonio were consuming their really excellent meal. The one or two glasses…well, three or four, if she was to be strictly honest…were helping to an-aesthetise her desperately unhappy heart.

She obviously *must* tell him that she had now dis-covered the truth. That she had put them both through the tortures of hell only because she'd been utterly blind and stupid.

But he already knew that, didn't he? He'd *always* known that he was innocent of those terrible accusa-tions she'd made against him. So he was hardly going to be interested to know that she'd seen the light—at last! Other than to be able to point out—at some length, and as cruelly hurtfully as he felt inclined— just what an idiot she'd been.

And she'd have to take it on the chin. Because she deserved it. Even a grovelling apology on her part wasn't going to make any difference to the way he felt about her.

On top of which…Antonio had, after his long soak in the bath, changed into more comfortable, casual clothes for their informal supper. Unfortunately, he'd chosen to put on a soft black cashmere sweater over a black open-necked silk shirt. Which was definitely *not* helpful, since he was looking even more handsome and diabolically attractive than usual.

Her other major problem…was that huge bed!

'Never mind, *querida*,' he murmured now, his dark eyes glinting with amusement as he caught her giving a slightly nervous glance at the bed. 'At least there will be plenty of room for both of us to have a good sleep without disturbing one another, hmm?' he added, his cool tone of voice throwing cold water over the slightly feverish thoughts which she'd been unable to stop flickering through her mind.

You fool! she told herself roughly. Why should he want *you*? Especially now that he's undoubtedly got that voluptuous Carlotta Perez keeping him warm at night!

But Antonio—who must have recently taken up clairvoyance, she told herself grimly—seemed to have no problem in reading her mind.

'You made a reference, earlier this evening, to Carlotta,' he drawled, staring down at the tall champagne flute in front of him and slowly revolving the stem between his long, slim, tanned fingers.

'In fact,' he added slowly, still avoiding her gaze as he stared down at the golden bubbles in his glass, 'I must admit to feeling deeply insulted that you should think that I would have anything to do with a woman who caused you—and subsequently myself—such deep unhappiness.'

'But…but I saw a photograph of you both, in that magazine,' she protested, suddenly feeling slightly disorientated by the low, deep note of sincerity in his voice. 'It was only natural… I mean, what else could

I think about the two of you? That picture was very…explicit.'

Antonio shrugged his shoulders before raising his head to give her a slightly bitter, twisted smile.

'It was taken some months ago at a wine-tasting. And was undoubtedly just a piece of bravado on her part, for the camera. But—who knows? Because Carlotta no longer works for my company. In fact, I have no idea what she is doing nowadays.'

There was a long silence as she tried to digest what he'd been saying.

'I…er…I was very surprised, and, I freely admit, very upset, when I saw that picture in the magazine,' Gina murmured, throwing him a quick, cautious glance through her eyelashes. 'I found it hard to really believe, that you and she… Well, to tell you the truth I don't suppose I'd even have seen the cutting if Roxana hadn't sent it to me.' She gave a helpless shrug of her shoulders. 'Which is why I naturally assumed that…'

'*Roxana!*' he ground out angrily. 'Believe me, I'm going to *kill* that sister of mine. Just as soon as I can get my hands on her!'

'Not if I get there first you won't!' Gina told him grimly.

And then, as they caught each other's eyes, Antonio's lips began to twitch, and she couldn't prevent her own lips from curving into a wide, amused smile, before they both burst into loud peals of laughter.

Their shared amusement seemed to clear the air between them. And although she couldn't pretend that Antonio remained anything other than his recent, sternly controlled self, Gina was highly relieved to feel the heavy, ominous dark cloud lifting slightly from her slim shoulders.

However, by the time their meal was over—and it was clearly time for bed—she once again found herself prey to increasing nervous strain and apprehension.

As Antonio stripped off the black cashmere sweater and began unbuttoning his black silk shirt she distractedly waved aside his suggestion that she might wish to use their communal bathroom.

'No, you go first,' she muttered, picking up a magazine she'd been reading on the plane and trying to avoid looking at Antonio as he removed his shirt and began undoing the zip of his trousers.

Unfortunately, there was nothing she could do to control the increasingly rapid beat of her heart as his naked figure walked casually past her towards their *en suite* bathroom.

Glancing fleetingly through her eyelashes at the broad, powerful strength of his shoulders and muscular arms made her feel quite weak. And it was only when he turned and closed the door behind him that she felt able to relax and try to pull herself together.

Goodness knows how she was going to get through this night, she told herself miserably. Because she *still* couldn't seem to handle the effect that Antonio had on her—both in bed and out of it.

By the time he'd returned to the bedroom, and was slipping naked between the sheets on the far side of the bed, she was in such a state of nervous tension that she practically bolted into the bathroom.

Maybe a shower might help to calm her down—and also take her mind off the unhappy prospect of spending a long, lonely night lying awake beside her husband. Or…or could this be her one last chance to try and save her marriage?

But by the time she'd washed her hair and was blowing dry the long, pale gold strands, she was in a total state of indecision. Swinging mentally this way and that, she simply couldn't decide what to do. The problem was that it was she who'd mentioned the dreaded word: divorce. If she attempted some sort of seduction then she would have to face the cruel possibility that he might reject her.

However, as she was brushing her now dry hair, Gina realised that she had to pull herself together.

Unfortunately, the one part of her mind which controlled reason and logic was lecturing her severely, telling herself not to be such an idiot as to court disaster. While the other, emotional half didn't appear to be taking a blind bit of notice. It was only concerned with carefully brushing her hair and dabbing her favourite scent on her pulse-points, before turning around and glancing critically at her naked body in the floor-to-ceiling mirror.

You do know that you're about to make an enormous fool of yourself, don't you? her sane, sensible mind warned her.

But the emotional sapphire-blue eyes were staring defiantly back at her in the mirror, clearly determined to take this very last possible chance of saving her marriage.

However, by the time she'd gathered up enough courage to leave the bathroom, Gina saw that Antonio had turned off his bedside light and was lying with his back to her, apparently fast asleep. The only light switched on in the room was that of her own bedside lamp, whose dim glow barely pierced the surrounding darkness.

Realising that she had probably spent too long in the bathroom, she hesitated for a moment in the open doorway. And then, giving a brief shrug of her slim shoulders, she moved silently across the carpet, slipping naked into bed beside Antonio.

Lying silently for a few moments, she was just about to turn off her own light when she realised that, although he might appear to be fast asleep, it was obvious from the slightly uneven rhythm of his breathing that her husband was still very much awake.

Taking a deep breath, she rolled carefully across the bed towards him and slowly put out a hand to touch him, very lightly, on the shoulder.

CHAPTER NINE

'ANTONIO...?' she whispered softly, gently resting the tips of her fingers on his broad shoulder.

'Hmm...?'

'I was just...er...just wondering if you were still awake?'

'Yes. Obviously,' he grunted.

'Oh...good.'

'Go to sleep, Gina,' he muttered.

'I can't. I'm not sleepy,' she murmured, her fingers moving very slowly, barely touching his skin.

'You've had a long journey. You must be tired.'

'Well, no...as it happens, I'm not.' She hesitated for a moment, allowing her fingers to trail gently down over his muscular back. 'But, of course, if *you* are feeling very tired...?'

'I did not say that,' he corrected her quietly in the darkness.

'No, you didn't,' she agreed, her fingertips continuing to move in a gentle, feather-light touch over his smooth, warm skin.

'I was merely concerned for you. It will be a long day tomorrow.'

'Yes, I know. But the thing is...I do want to talk to you.'

'Humph!'

She wasn't at all sure what that slight grunt signi-fied, but, encouraged by the fact that he hadn't moved away—or commented on the touch of her fingers, now

tracing delicate lazy patterns over the broad expanse
of his back—she decided to try and take another small
step forward.

'There is something that I want...that I need to say
to you,' she whispered softly.

'Oh, yes?'

'Umm...'

'And what is it that you need to say?' he murmured.

'Well...it is a little difficult...talking to your back,'
she pointed out quietly, before leaning forward to
gently press her warm lips to his shoulderblade, while
lowering her hand to rest it lightly on the curve of his
waist.

There was a long...a *very* long, heart-stopping silence, before Antonio eventually gave a deep, heavy
sigh.

'Very well, Gina,' he muttered, before slowly rolling on to his back.

Raising his arms and clasping his hands behind his
head, he settled himself comfortably back against the
pillows. 'What do you want to talk to me about?'

So far—so good! she told herself, feeling incredibly
nervous. But she wasn't under any illusion about the
difficulty she faced. The way he kept referring to her
by her Christian name, and not his usual, far more
affectionate night-time use of *'querida'* or 'darling'
was, quite frankly, an ominous sign.

'I...I felt I should say...if it isn't too late...that I
don't want a divorce,' she murmured softly, leaning
on her elbow and gazing down in the dim light at her
husband.

'Really?' he drawled. The expression on his face
was totally inscrutable, giving her no clue as to what
was going through his mind.

'No… That's not what I want at all.'

'And what *do* you want, Gina?'

'Well…' She took a deep breath to steady her nerves, allowing her free hand to settle lightly on his stomach.

'Well…as you can imagine, I've given our marriage a great deal of thought,' she began slowly. 'I was so much…so *very* much in love with you. So deeply and truly happy. Which is why I now think…why I'm now almost certain…that I simply couldn't cope with… with everything. With being told by Carlotta and your old uncle about the background to our wedding, for instance, only moments before I learned of my grandfather's death.'

'Yes, I, too, have been aware of that fact for some time,' he told her quietly.

'But…but you never said anything?'

'Why do you think I didn't ask you for a divorce long ago? Why would I have put up with such unhappiness and torment if I hadn't believed you to be half out of your mind with grief?'

'Oh, Antonio…!' She shut her eyes for a moment against the weak tears which were threatening to fall at any moment. 'I've been *such* a fool!'

'I won't disagree with that statement!' he told her grimly.

'But…I've now had time to think about…er…what happened,' she said, hesitantly trailing her fingers over his flat stomach, one half of her mind noting the instinctive clenching of his muscles at her touch as she tried to gather enough courage to say what must be said.

'The thing is…well, I don't know how to say this…but I only learned today that all those terrible things I said—those really *awful* accusations I threw at you about only marrying me for my money—were totally untrue!'

'Well, well!' he said mockingly. 'Is that the reason behind your sudden appearance here in Spain?'

She stared down at him for a moment, tempted to take the easy route out of her difficulty, but finally forced herself to shake her head.

'No...I'm afraid that I haven't even got the excuse of dropping everything in London to rush here and beg your pardon. Although I *am* trying to ask for your forgiveness, of course,' she admitted sorrowfully.

'The fact is,' she continued with a heavy sigh, 'Roxana begged me so hard and so long to come to her wedding that I finally agreed to do so. And it was only when I arrived, and got around to reading the letter from my lawyer which arrived at the house in London this morning, that the scales finally fell from my eyes.'

'Well, at least that is an honest answer.' He shrugged. 'I must confess that I have been wondering whether you had received the letter from my lawyers. And when—*if at all*—you would get around to acknowledging the fact.'

'Oh, Antonio—do be fair!' she protested. 'I may have been stupid, and hurtful, and...and behaved most cruelly to you. But you *must* know that I would never, *ever* try to brush everything under the carpet. Not once I'd learned that my wild accusations were total moonshine!'

'Maybe not,' he agreed slowly. 'But that letter was sent by my lawyers well over a month ago.'

'Yes, well, I know that *now*,' she told him earnestly. 'But my lawyer wrote to say that he's been in hospital, for an operation…I can show you his letter, if you like…and that's why I only heard today.'

'Ah, well…' He gave a heavy sigh.

'The thing is,' she added hurriedly, 'I really do owe you the most fulsome and abject apology. I…I really can't believe that I've been such an idiot all these months. In fact, I can hardly bear to recall even half the terrible things I said to you. And…and when you accused me of not having faith and trust in you—you were absolutely right. I was stupid, and selfish, and…and…'

'It's all right, *querida*,' he told her softly.

'No, it's not,' she snapped nervously. 'I've still got a lot of things to say. And if you keep on interrupting I'll lose my train of thought!'

'Ah, yes—of course. Forgive me,' he murmured, doing his best to keep a straight face, but unable to prevent his dark eyes from gleaming with amusement.

'I know you're laughing at me—you damn man!' she told him crossly. 'But I *am* trying to apologise, and to confess how desperately sorry I am about my horrid behaviour.'

'You're absolutely right,' he assured her solemnly. 'I am a great believer in confession. It's supposed to be good for the soul, I understand.'

'Well…I'd be grateful if you'd just shut up and let me get on with it,' she ground out, in a thoroughly un-loverlike tone of voice. 'Now, where was I?'

'That is a very good question.' He grinned. 'How about pressing the "fast forward" button and coming straight to the bit where you tell me that, despite everything which has happened, you still love me more than life itself?'

'"More than life itself"? Hmm…I think that might

be going just a *little* too far,' she teased, trailing her fingers up over his deeply tanned skin, through the curly dark hair covering his broad chest, and back down the slim line of hair leading past his waist towards his manhood.

'But I'm happy to talk about how much I love and need you,' she added softly. 'Far from wanting a divorce, I want to stay married to you for the rest of my days. If that's all right with you, of course...?'

'Yes, I don't think I have a problem with that,' he murmured. 'However, while I hate to interrupt this "talk" of yours, I have to confess that I am finding the touch of your hand extremely...er...distracting.'

'No! Really?' She turned her head to gaze at him, her blue eyes wide with well-simulated surprise.

'Hmm...yes, I fear so,' he told her, his lips twitching with laughter. 'Although I do find myself wondering—strange as it may seem—whether you could possibly be attempting to seduce me?'

'Me? Seduce you?' She gave a low, breathless laugh. 'Darling Antonio—how could I *possibly* do anything like that? I'm English, for heaven's sake!'

'Ah, yes. I must have forgotten that important fact,' he drawled.

'And I need hardly remind you,' she said, slowly slipping her hand down beneath the sheet, towards the matt of dark, curly hair at the apex of his thighs, 'that nice, well brought-up English women would *never* dream of doing anything so extraordinarily out of character!'

'No...no, of course not,' he agreed, before she heard him gave a slight catch of breath as her fingers discovered that he was already strongly aroused.

Ah! So maybe her cool, controlled husband wasn't

quite as calm and nonchalant as he might like her to think, Gina told herself, surprised to discover that she was enjoying playing the part of a wicked seductress.

It was a completely new role for her, of course, since Antonio had always been very much the dominant figure in their lovemaking. And she'd been more than happy to leave the initiative to him. But now...well, maybe it was time to turn the tables? To see if she could shake that strong iron control of his?

'As I recall, you were saying a few moments ago how much you loved and needed me,' he said blandly, not betraying by a flicker of an eyelid the fact that they were both aware of her increasingly intimate touch. 'Perhaps you'd like to tell me more about that?'

'Well, the truth is that I fell quite madly and hopelessly in love with you, my darling Antonio, the very first moment I set eyes on you, when I was only eighteen,' she confessed. 'And there's never been anyone else of any importance in my life since then.'

'Hmm...I'm glad to hear it,' he murmured huskily, as his flesh swelled and hardened beneath her soft touch.

'Which is why...why I totally lost my cool—and all control—when you suddenly turned up in Suffolk,' she admitted, slowly lowering her head to press light kisses to the rough hair on his broad chest, before trailing her lips down his strong body, her long fair hair brushing enticingly over his skin.

'And then...when you made love to me...' she murmured, her mouth and hands exploring every inch of his skin, her own pleasure increasing as she felt the deep muscles of his torso and stomach tense and contract beneath her soft touch. 'When you made love to me…I was in such total, utter heaven that I'd have followed you to the ends of the earth, if need be.'

'Ah, my darling! I felt exactly the same,' he murmured, swiftly removing his hands from behind his dark head and cradling her blond head in the palms of his hands as he drew her up towards him, possessing her mouth gently at first, and then with an increasing depth of passion which left her breathless with desire.

As he gradually released his firm grip, she again began trailing her lips slowly down over his muscular chest, savouring the spicy aroma of his cologne and the musky masculine scent of his body. She was caught up by a thrilling feeling of power, astonished by the sheer excitement and delight of hearing the sound of his increasingly ragged breath, the soft groan breaking involuntarily from his throat, provoked by the sweet torment of her hands and lips moving delicately over the most sensitive, vulnerable part of his anatomy.

And then…as if unable to bear any more of the exquisite, lingering torture…a deep shudder seemed to shake his tall frame as, with a fierce growl, he swiftly rolled her over, pinning her to the mattress with his long, hard body.

'Enough! I have been without the pleasure of your soft body for too long!' he ground out impatiently, and she was humbled as she became aware of his strong body trembling and shaking, struggling to control his passionate need for her. And then she was only conscious of a frenzied excitement, eagerly welcoming him as he swiftly and smoothly drove himself into her, the powerful, hard thrusts of his body a dark, rhythmic beat that seemed to carry them both up and over the edge of the world, before they found themselves free-falling slowly back to earth.

Much later, as they lay together in a tangle of sheets, their limbs entwined with one another, she slowly surfaced from a drowsy languor to feel him gently running his fingers through the coils of her long fair hair.

'How I love you, my darling!' he murmured softly. 'So much—and for so long.'

'But...but you haven't said so,' she muttered, struggling to sit up. 'Not for a long time. Not since our honeymoon,' she added sorrowfully.

'But, yes—you must have known how I felt?' he protested. 'Surely you understood—even those nights when I came to you so late and so secretly—surely you *must* have understood my great need of you? Did you not understand that every time I took you into my arms I was demonstrating just how much I love and desire you?'

Gina shook her head. 'I was clearly out of my mind, wasn't I? In fact, I obviously couldn't see one inch beyond my own nose. How could I have been such an idiot? To have been looking down the wrong end of the telescope all this while. What a waste of time to have been so terribly unhappy these last months.'

'It's all a matter of trust, my darling. As I told myself—you should have *known* that I am not the sort of man to be a fortune-hunter. I was most deeply hurt. And, I'm sorry to say, furiously angry that you could believe that I would *ever* behave in such a way. Or to think such thoughts about your grandfather, come to that. Because he loved you most sincerely. And you really should have known that, too.'

Gina gave a heavy sigh. 'You're quite right, of

course. I seem to have made a complete mess of just about everything. Even going so far as to believe that your poor old uncle Emilio was involved in our marriage. I must have been completely out of my mind for the past few months!'

'Well...' Antonio hesitated for a moment. 'You were wrong, of course. But not entirely so, I'm afraid.'

'What do you mean?'

He gave a heavy sigh. 'It has taken me some time to fit all the pieces of the puzzle together—and it was your grandfather's secretary, Margaret, who gave me the final clue to the puzzle.'

'The final clue...to what puzzle?' she demanded impatiently.

'The question of why my uncle was so convinced that he and your grandfather had arranged our marriage. When of course we both know that they did not.'

'So—what really happened?'

'Ah...well, as far as I can see, it goes something like this...' Antonio said, putting an arm about her slim figure and holding her close to his warm body.

'I must remind you, first of all, that my uncle did not willingly give up the reins of our family business. He had always been a total autocrat, running the company in his own individual way and brooking no outside interference.'

'Yes, I had gathered that.'

'So, when his heart condition became serious, and the doctors told him he must let go, he bitterly resented having to do so. Although I must in all fairness admit that he tried to be philosophical about the situation,' Antonio pointed out. 'However, it was clearly hard for him. And he was also very concerned that I was unmarried—that I had not yet provided a son and heir to carry on the family name.

'And, being an imperious old man, he would constantly press me to get married, and if possible to a woman with a rich dowry—just as he had done, so many years ago. However, I had made it quite clear, many times, that I was not interested in marrying for any reason other than love. Particularly as I had already fallen deeply and irrevocably in love some years before, and was not prepared to accept second best. So—we had a stalemate between us.'

'You mentioned this woman once before. When you first arrived in Suffolk,' she said, stirring restlessly in his embrace. 'I can't pretend that I'm happy about it. But I think you'd better tell me all about her, don't you?'

'All in good time,' he promised. 'However, to return to my story. The event which acted as a catalyst was the visit I made to London in search of my missing shipment of wine. You need to know that my uncle was—and is—a smart, tough old man, with a good memory. And he had been a long-time friend of your grandfather, with whom he'd done business for many years. I'd told him that Brandon's were responsible for the shipment being missing. So, as soon as I left for a quick trip around Europe before travelling to London, he got straight on the phone to your grandfather.'

'Why on earth did he do that?' she queried with a frown.

'Because he knew that Sir Robert was not just as old and as infirm as he was but that he was also very wealthy, and that he had an orphan granddaughter— the heiress to his entire estate. And, above all, because he was determined to prove to me—and maybe the world—that while he might be old, he was still a force to be reckoned with. Incidentally,' Antonio added with a shrug, 'my uncle has admitted to everything that I've said so far.'

'But that's daft!' she protested. 'For all your uncle knew, I could have been married with a whole tribe of children!'

'Which is why he phoned your grandfather—to discover the current situation. And it was then that those two old men decided to put their heads together and see if they couldn't somehow arrange a marriage between us.'

'So, it really *was* all a plot between them after all?' she exclaimed.

Antonio shook his head. 'No. Not in the way you mean. Because, of course, it's just not possible to force anyone into a marriage if they are unwilling to go along with the scheme. So, what those two old men actually did was, in fact, rather clever. Because, after quizzing Margaret, I now know that the "missing shipment" had already been located in Bristol—long before I reached London.'

'Are you trying to tell me that all that searching through those dusty cellars in Ipswich was a complete and utter waste of our time?' she demanded indignantly.

'Got it in one!' Antonio laughed. 'All your grandfather could do—and you must admit he did it very well—was give us the opportunity to meet each other again. He either suspected, or had a very good idea, that you and I had been involved in some sort of romance when you were much younger. So he spun this yarn about the shipment probably being up in Suffolk, and why didn't I go up and check it out for myself? However, just to make sure that I had to spend at least *one* night up there, he took me back to his house for lunch—where he managed to spin out the meal for some hours—so that it was very late in the afternoon by the time I left London. And then he just sat back and waited to see what happened!'

'So…so he and your uncle really *did* sort of arrange our marriage,' she said slowly.

'Yes—but not in the way you supposed. When I returned with you, at the end of the long weekend, to ask his permission to marry you, I have to say that your grandfather seemed almost shocked to begin with.' Antonio laughed. 'Quite honestly, my darling, I don't think even *he* had ever imagined that his scheme would prove to be quite so successful! Although I can promise you that neither then nor later did he make *any* mention of the money he was intending to leave me. You have my solemn word on that. In fact, I now know from my uncle that the two old men arranged that little item between them.'

'OK…I can just about see what happened—and my grandfather certainly had a *real* stroke of luck with our housekeeper and her husband being away for the weekend. You don't know Doris Lambert,' Gina added with a laugh. 'But I can assure you there would have been absolutely *no* mad lovemaking sessions going on if *she'd* been around!'

'Ah, my darling,' he murmured, pressing a kiss on her brow. 'Whatever the difficulty, I would have somehow found a way into your bed.'

'But what about this woman whom you fell in love with all those years ago? You haven't yet told me about her.'

'Really, Gina—how can you be so obtuse?' He grinned, shaking his head in mock exasperation. 'It was *you*, of course. I met you when I was twenty-six and you were only just eighteen—and far too young to cope with a fully adult love affair. Indeed, I was bitterly ashamed that it went even as far as it did.'

'Which was precisely nowhere!' she retorted. 'Even though I would have gone to bed with you like a shot, given half a chance. But all I had to sustain me over the next eight years was one measly kiss!'

'You're damned lucky that's all it was!' he growled, clasping her tightly in his arms. 'I had the devil's own problems keeping my hands off you. Because it was clear that you were very young for your age, and also very innocent. So I knew that I had to wait for you to grow up.

'In fact, when I found myself driving up to Suffolk, I was a prey to all sorts of fears and doubts,' Antonio said slowly. 'It had been a long time. You could have changed out of all recognition. You might not care for me anymore. And, indeed, I might discover that my feelings had changed as well. However, I couldn't resist finding out what had happened to the lovely young girl with whom I'd unfortunately fallen in love all those years ago. A girl who was so young and untouched. And who'd haunted my mind and body for a long, long time.'

'Really?' Gina beamed at him. 'Really and truly?'

He laughed. 'Yes, I'm afraid so. Although I did my best to forget her. Even going so far as to become briefly engaged some years ago. However, none of my romances ever really came to a satisfactory conclusion. Nor, incidentally, did I *ever* have an affair with

Carlotta Perez. And if she claimed I did, it was solely in her head. I hope you believe me, *querida*.'

'Yes, of course I do.'

'And I did not understand why I was never satisfied with any other women—until I found myself running across a lawn to rescue a girl with long, long blonde hair from a bolting horse.'

'Except Pegasus was *not* bolting,' she reminded him firmly. 'Just anxious to get back to his stable!'

'So you told me at the time—and very fiercely, too!' he laughed. 'But I still found you absolutely enchanting! And once I held you again in my arms...as I'd done so long ago in Seville...I immediately found myself falling in love with you all over again.'

'Oh, wow! That's *so* romantic!' Gina sighed happily.

'I don't know about romantic. At the time, it felt as if I'd been struck by a savage bolt of lightning. And yet I knew—at that very moment—that there would never be anyone else for me, either in this life or for all eternity.'

'Oh, darling!' Gina murmured, staring at him with misty eyes. 'That's absolutely the loveliest thing anyone's *ever* said to me.'

'And although we have had many problems in our short marriage,' he said softly, 'we will do better in the future, *no*?'

'Yes,' she whispered, as his arms closed possessively about her. 'Yes, we will. Because I love you, Antonio, with all my heart.'

'And I love you, my darling. I intend to love and cherish you all the days of my life,' he breathed huskily, his lips claiming hers in a long, ardent kiss of total commitment.

VIVA LA VIDA DE AMOR!

They speak the language of passion.

In Harlequin Presents®, you'll find a special kind of lover—full of Latin charm. Whether he's relaxing in denims or dressed for dinner, giving you diamonds or simply sweet dreams, he's got spirit, style and sex appeal!

Latin Lovers is the new miniseries from Harlequin Presents® for anyone who enjoys hot romance!

Meet gorgeous Antonio Scarlatti in
THE BLACKMAILED BRIDEGROOM
by Miranda Lee, Harlequin Presents® #2151
available January 2001

And don't miss sexy Niccolo Dominici in
THE ITALIAN GROOM
by Jane Porter, Harlequin Presents® #2168
available March 2001!

Available wherever Harlequin books are sold.

HARLEQUIN®
Makes any time special™

He's a man of cool sophistication.
He's got pride, power and wealth.
He's a ruthless businessman, an expert lover—
and he's one hundred percent committed
to staying single.

Until now. Because suddenly he's responsible
for a BABY!

HIS BABY

An exciting miniseries from Harlequin Presents®
**He's sexy, he's successful…
and now he's facing up to fatherhood!**

On sale February 2001:
RAFAEL'S LOVE-CHILD
by Kate Walker, Harlequin Presents® #2160

On sale May 2001:
MORGAN'S SECRET SON
by Sara Wood, Harlequin Presents® #2180

And look out for more later in the year!

Available wherever Harlequin books are sold.

HARLEQUIN®
Makes any time special ™

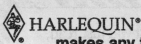

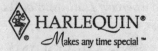